In memory:

My neighbor Archie Dunaway
and all other warriors who were martyred
for serving the Lord

Other Books by the Author

Fire Mission! Fire Mission! A Forward Observer's Experiences in Vietnam. Captain Larry Kenneth Hunter
The Bethlehem Midwife

CONTENTS

CHAPTER 1

THE BATTLE

Jay waited intently behind the crouched, Kevlar-covered figures in front of him and hoped everyone remembered the briefing notes.

He whispered, "Polite, are you in position?"

Two swear words came through his earpiece, letting him know that his sniper had the rooftop and second floor windows covered.

It was time. He tapped the man in front who relayed it to the person in front of him, who tapped the two holding the battering ram. They jumped forward and smashed the ram just below the doorknob. It ripped and flung open. The two rolled to the right side of the door frame, allowing a flashbang to be tossed in. Everyone instinctively closed their eyes to protect their vision, and after the explosion, the man in front of Jay went in low to the right, while Jay dove in to the left with his AR at the ready and safety now off.

Looking into the darkened warehouse, he searched for any shadowy figures immediately in front of him. He heard some startled yells, but they seemed more distant. He looked for cover and found an old generator that he crouched behind. With the element of surprise lost, he heard automatic fire open up and smash into the door as the rest of his team charged in. He had hoped they would all make it in, but he heard a grunt of pain as a bullet struck below the Kevlar vest, and the last one in stumbled to the floor. He raised and saw a flicker of light on the first crosswalk on the second floor. He fired a long burst of fire at the area, and while extravagant on ammunition, it was necessary to keep that terrorist's head down so everyone could find shelter. He wasn't sure if he hit him, but the firing from there stopped and allowed the others to spread to the sidewalls. Taking turns, partners would fire, allowing the back man to advance and then change out magazines while he fired in turn.

When he heard covering fire beside him, he darted forward to the cover of an old conveyor belt he remembered from the diagram they had reviewed. Peeking up, he noticed the fire from the first crosswalk had stopped and was confident someone had taken out that threat. He rose a little higher where he could see at the end of the warehouse an office on the second-story platform and the two stairways from the shop floor on either end. The office was where they were anticipating the hostage was held, and he hoped everyone remembered not to confuse their flashbangs with their grenades in the office itself.

Seeing flickers of light that seemed to be directed at him he called out, "Spelchek, do you see two shooters on the second cross-walk just before the office?"

Above the chatter of the machine guns, he heard, "Yeah."

"Can you take them?"

"Negative, no clear shot, too much cover."

Stumped, Jay thought out loud, "Can you bounce a rifle grenade off the wall behind them?"

Shortly, he heard a whomp as Spelchek fired up and over the crosswalk. There was a loud boom and silence from the crosswalk.

"Yes," he yelled, as he and Spelchek scrambled toward the stairwell on the left, knowing that the others would be headed to the right. He slid along the wall with his AR pointed up at the top of the stairs. Suddenly, a round object came bouncing down the stairs.

"Grenade!" he yelled, as he closed his eyes and dove behind the stairs. An explosion pushed him sideways and even with his eyes closed and ear buds in, he was partially blinded and deafened. He pushed himself off the ground and craned his head looking up the stairwell. Movement at the opening opposite the stairs caught his eye, and he unloaded his AR until two tracers showed he had reached half of his magazine, so he sprayed the other half of the magazine at the roof above him hoping they would find a mark.

He dropped the magazine, reloaded, and called out, "Spelchek, cover me." Looking back, he wasn't reassured as a dusty Spelchek nodded okay but looked groggy, and his gun wasn't pointed up. Jay feinted with his head and gun out on the stairwell. Receiving no fire, he ran in a crouch halfway, just far enough to lob a flashbang over the edge and duck his head back down. After the burst of light that he could see through his closed eyes, he charged up the rest of the way and glanced left and right. It was immediately reassuring to see a body down where he had emptied his magazine through the floor. He spun to the left and looked right but didn't see anyone. He could hear Spelchek clank up the stairs and take up right point. He pointed to the office building, and they both walked carefully in that direction, scanning in all directions and Spelchek covering his six.

He dipped his head around the corner and saw a guard sprawled in front of the door. Movement on the other side of the building almost caused him to fire as adrenaline was surging through his mind and trigger finger. Only strict discipline kept him from firing before confirming his target, and he was relieved that he hadn't fired as it was Rhino on the other side.

"Is your side clear?" Jay whispered over his mic.

"Yes, but I lost Gundam coming up the stairs."

Jay grimaced as this would make it harder trying to breach the office with only three men now. He motioned for Spelchek to cover him, and he crawled under the window, over the body to the door. After making sure his partners were covering him, he reached behind his back and pulled out "the snake." Carefully unrolling the fiber optic coil, he turned on the five-millimeter scope and looked to make sure the optics weren't broken as he looked in the eyepiece. There were only about six black dots to show damage after the explosion, and he could still see fairly clear. He tried to slide "the snake" under the door, but it had too tight a seal. With his back to the wall, he slithered back to the window and held the scope up to a corner. It wasn't an optimal view, but at least the window was uncovered. In the dark, he could see someone in a chair in the far left corner, which he assumed was the hostage and two armed people standing on either side facing the door. While sweeping the room from the bottom of the window, he didn't understand when his view went black. He looked at the power button and then checked to see if the scope was still plugged in. Everything seemed correct; when he looked back through the eyepiece, glints of light lit up a bandolier of ammunition, and his heart stopped when he realized someone was up against the window above him, looking out.

He carefully pulled the snake down, looked right and left at Rhino and Spelchek, and held up three fingers. Two he pointed over either shoulder while looking at Rhino, while the third he raised over his head and nodded at Spelchek who nodded back.

Hugging the wall, he crawled back to Rhino, and he looked back at Spelchek who immediately opened up, shooting at chest height through the window and shattering it. He and Rhino hammered the door as Spelchek dropped a flashbang in. At least he hoped it was a flashbang and not a grenade or the hostage would be dead, and all this effort would be wasted. The distraction worked as the door flew open. He rolled right and fired high at the right-sided guard while Rhino took down the one on the left.

Jay charged toward the hostage in case there was a dead man's trigger, but both guards were down with empty hands. While Jay swept the rest of the room, he heard Rhino yell, "Look out."

The guard Spelchek had downed through the window rolled over, pulled a pin, and threw a grenade into the corner. Jay reacted without thinking and hurled his body over the grenade.

There was a thunderous explosion, and everything went red and then black.

"You Are Dead," flashed across the console screen and reflected red light across Jay's glasses.

"Mission Complete."

Jay could hear cheering from his teammates through his headphones.

"We did it! Good job, guys. I didn't get many points from that round, but I know I can level up and catch up with your rank."

Spelchek laughed. "In your dreams."

Suddenly, even through his headphones, Jay could hear his little sister whine, "Mom, Jay's still playing computer games, and it's ten thirty."

His mother stuck her head in Jay's room. Wearing his purple Dr. Who T-shirt and black jeans, it was difficult to see Jay in his custom-designed swivel chair in the darkened room.

"Jay, it's a school night."

Jay's mildly spiked hair was matted flat in the back from long-term use of his headset, but he lifted one side of his headphones to show he was listening.

"Yes, ma'am, just one more round."

"Okay," his mother replied. "Now, Angela, go to sleep."

A short time later, after a couple more rounds, Jay was shocked to see it was eleven thirty. "Guys, I'm sorry but I really have to go," and against their protests, he carefully hung up his headphones and shut down the computer. He tiptoed to the bathroom, carefully avoiding the creaky floorboard and went to bed.

CHAPTER 2

THE WARRIORS

Zero degrees

The next morning, Jay fumbled futilely at his cell phone as it belligerently blared an ear-piercing klaxon. The third attempt finally killed it, and he glared at the blinking "6:00." He looked at his Bible, but hit snooze and thought, *I'm not getting up at this unholy hour.*

Immediately, he found himself standing in a large mission control room where a large floating earth rotated in the center. The orb was about two stories tall and portrayed in crisp, clear 3-D details that he had never seen from any satellite image. It wasn't a hologram but solid and improbably suspended in the air. All over it were red blinking lights. Most sprang up and went out but some pulsed strong and steady. Between Jay and the globe were multiple consoles with hologram screens staffed by people working intently and with purpose.

Jay sensed the presence of a person standing beside him. He turned to his right and saw an imposing man standing with a rigid military bearing. A reflective glare bounced off his ebony skin and sharp brown eyes. Jay squinted his eyes with concern and asked him, "Sir, is this NASA mission control or NORAD? Have the Russians launched a nuclear attack?"

"Jay, this is the prayer processing center," the man replied.

Jay gawked at him confusedly. "Who are you?"

"You may call me Stallworth, and you have been brought here for a purpose."

Jay just noticed Stallworth's uniform, which didn't have any flag patches to identify which country he served with. Jay was familiar with every major military uniform from his hours online, but this one was completely unknown. However, Stallworth's confident command presence and short cropped hair seemed to indicate he was military.

Baffled, Jay shook his head.

"This must be a dream," he muttered. "That pizza from the fridge last night must have been older than I thought."

The man reached out and pinched Jay's triceps with an iron grip.

"Does that feel like a dream?"

"Hey, easy there," Jay yelped, as he tried to twist out of his grip. The man let go.

"Jay, listen up and learn. What do you see?"

"I see a lot of people typing on computers and looking up at this big globe," Jay replied.

"What do you think they are doing?" Stallworth asked.

"I have no idea." Jay shook his head trying to clear up his confusion.

"They're recording every prayer sent up to God," Stallworth explained and waved his hand over the hive of activity.

Jay stared more closely at the slowly rotating world and realized that he could pick out Europe directly above him and Africa mostly below him. He discovered the two of them were standing on an elevated platform level with the equator. On the globe, there was a straight dividing line running from the North Pole to South Pole, separating the dark half on the left from the bright right hemisphere, which the sun's rays were presently illuminating. The world was cocked on its axis so most of Africa and Europe were in the golden sunlight, but the Atlantic Ocean and Great Britain were still in darkness.

Red strobes, like laser beams, blinked on and off over the two continents regularly, but Jay could rarely see any flashing on the dark blue oceans.

Jay watched as the light progressed across the land mass, and as it advanced, a random pattern of red beacons blinked on in that rim of weak sunlight. In front of him, Jay saw a person hunched over his console with a globe replica before him. As the red lights popped up on the world in front of him, the person clicked a stylus on a light, which opened an image of an African speaking on his computer console. As dozens of workers opened up these icons on their consoles, a flood of French speakers started coming through, as well as many African dialects, predominantly from West Africa.

"What do these lights represent?" Jay asked, pointing at the heaviest concentration over Nigeria.

"Each light represents a prayer being offered up by a believer, and it is our job to tabulate and record them."[1]

"I thought God could hear every prayer being offered up immediately," Jay protested.

"Yes, that's true," Stallworth agreed. "He doesn't need this, but it's a blessing for us to participate in His purpose and plan. This duty is a privilege as we get to see His love and care for His children."

As Jay continued to look baffled, Stallworth switched the console to English subtitles. Immediately, the prayers were translated simultaneously beneath the person speaking. Jay was impressed as there didn't seem to be a lag time.

"You know He loves to hear his children praise him in their own heart language, but for your sake we will add subtitles," Stallworth clarified.

Like Zoom, video after video appeared on the dozens of consoles of people speaking in the bustling cities of Gambia, Liberia, Nigeria, and France. Just as the people were varied in their clothing and age, so were their multitude of postures while praying with some standing, others bowing and still some sitting. All were united in praising God the Father, Jesus Christ His Son, and the Holy Spirit. From

---

[1] Psalm 56:8.

the sweltering equatorial jungles to the dry desert, from the humid seacoast to the frosty fjords, men, women, and children of many nationalities raised their voices, and as they did, red lights popped up on the globe and were duly recorded. In many of the videos, a rosy pink tint could be seen in the sky promising the dawn of new day.

As the sunshine slowly plodded west, it touched the shores of the United Kingdom, and more English started filtering in through the bubbling noise. Cockney, Welsh, Scottish, and later, Irish accents started filling the room. Jay was glad that the English subtitles were still on as he generally couldn't make heads or tails on what was being said, but he appreciated the passion and fervor.

"What do you see?" Stallworth challenged him again.

Observing the progressing wave of red lights marching west across the United Kingdom and Ireland, Jay said, "The heaviest concentration of people praying seems to be just as the dawn has passed."

"You're correct," Stallworth noted. "Why do you think that is?"

"Well, I guess that's when the most Christians are praying," Jay replied.

"Yes, although prayers are lifted up throughout the day, it is the dawn when there are more prayers of praise and petition being raised to their Maker. This is indeed the Holy Hour of the day," Stallworth confirmed.

"David and Daniel are good examples of men who offered their prayers early in the morning. Christians worldwide continue to start their day by following the example of Jesus Christ who found a secluded spot early each morning to talk with His Father.

"Every morning, wherever Christians pray to the Father, that spot becomes Holy Ground, and a red beacon is launched up. We capture and record those prayers as well as the answers to them.

"On Saturdays and Sundays, we see our heaviest concentrations of prayer as people celebrate at places of worship all over the world. However, this Monday is typical for a weekday."

To Jay, it seemed that as the sunshine moved forward, it lit up the lasers like a fireworks display. He recalled what Stallworth said earlier and asked, "Why am I here?"

"Jay, have you read in the Bible that the angels in heaven are divided up into legions with a commander?"

"Yes, like the old Roman legions. I've always wondered about that."

"Well, Jay, then you remember each one of these legions was further subdivided into groups of a hundred, led by a centurion."

Jay nodded. "Like our regiments today are led by a colonel and then subdivided into four companies, each led by a captain."

"Yes, but did you know that under a centurion his cohort was broken down into groups of ten legionnaires led by a decurion?"

"No, I didn't know that. So would that be about the same as a lieutenant commanding a platoon?"

"Similar but a little smaller, more like a sergeant as a squad leader. The Father values order, which is why after the battle with the Amalekites, Jethro told Moses he needed to put officials in charge of thousands, hundreds, fifties, and tens.[2] As you know, we are battling for the souls of men at this time, and it is important to be organized. Although Jesus Christ won the war when he died on the cross, the deceiver is trying to steal as many souls as he can to join him when he is thrown into the pit."

Jay nodded. "But what does that have to do with me?"

Stallworth answered, "You've been recommended as a candidate for the position of decurion."

Jay's jaw dropped, and when he could get it working again, he said, "You want me to be a decurion commanding angels? Based on what?"

"Well, we have noticed you play a number of games on the internet…"

"You've been spying on me!" Jay accused.

"We monitor and record everything," Stallworth corrected. "NSA has nothing compared to us." He swept his arm out to encompass the busy computer terminals.

This subdued Jay as he looked at the globe and the hundreds of console screens and thought back to a few things he had done, which in looking back he wished hadn't been recorded.

---

[2] Exodus 18 17–23.

Bouncing back, he joked, "So is it my lightning fast reflexes and superior shooting skills that landed me up here."

Stallworth didn't crack a smile. "Your reflexes are just above average, but you have spent so much time on the computer your shooting skills are finally in the moderate to good category."

Jay glanced at Stallworth sharply and wondered, "Did he just slam me?"

"But your small unit leadership skills are quite good as you encourage others to play well together. You are getting to be a decent tactician, but the fact you are willing to put the mission above your personal satisfaction and rank has caught His attention."

Jay wanted to ask just whose attention, but with the confident way Stallworth declared this, he knew he was supposed to know.

"There are several other qualities necessary for a decurion, and we will see if you have what it takes."

"Is this a recruitment process like *The Last Starfighter*? I liked the storyline, but the graphics were terrible, or are we talking about something like *Men in Black*?" Jay asked. "If this is heaven, am I dead?'

"No, no," Stallworth reassured him. "You aren't dead yet, and the process is nothing like that. You have other abilities we need to measure and refine. Let me introduce you to your centurion."

Stallworth led him to a row of eleven consoles where there was a central console, which had a double wide screen bigger than all the others and an empty seat next to it.

"Excuse me, Centurion, if I might have a moment of your time."

The centurion turned around and shocked Jay. She was a small, spry lady with bobbed gray hair, who stared at him like he was an undesirable insect pinned on a tray.

"Centurion Julian, this is Jay Wright who will be joining us as a trainee. I appreciate you helping him to learn his duties," Stallworth said.

"Commander, I'll do it, but you know that we have the Dawn Patrol today."

"I understand, but you are the best at introducing new recruits to our expectations," Stallworth said. He glanced at Jay. "She taught kindergarten for thirty-seven years before becoming a centurion. She should be commanding a legion, but she's too good at what she does."

Centurion Julian peered hard at Jay, and he wondered how she could be so intimidating when she was six inches shorter than him.

"Can you take orders and obey them without question?" she asked abruptly.

"Yes, sir! Ma'am," he stammered. "I'm sorry what should I call you?"

"Centurion or Sister Julian."

"Sister Julie Anne?" he asked.

"No, Sister Julian," she emphasized. "That's another story. Let's go meet your team as it will help you understand your job and who you are communicating with at the console."

She walked down the rest of the row where people were feverishly tapping with styluses on their screens. They turned to the right and walked away from the rotating globe to a raised platform where a group of people were standing and talking.

Centurion Julian briskly took the two steps up the platform, "Dawn Patrol!"

"Centurion!" they answered back in unison, as they quickly shuffled into a straight line.

"This squad represents the best from my cohort and fulfills our motto 'To Glorify and Serve,'" the centurion explained. "Every message they carry, healing performed, person protected, and prayer answered is to the Glory of the Father, Son, and Holy Spirit."

Jay looked at the variety of figures gathered before him and was so shocked he blurted out, "I thought they would all be white."

From the group, Jay caught whispered words, "Racist," "Newbie," "Rookie," as well as growls and chirps of displeasure.

Centurion Julian queried him, "You thought they would all be white? What's your problem with Black and Brown people?"

"No, no," Jay protested. "I thought angels would all be wearing white robes with wings and looking identical."

"Do they look identical to you?" questioned the centurion. "Do you have a hard time telling Africans and Asians apart?"

Yasaka

"No, they don't look the same, and I can tell African Americans apart, I have friends who are African Americans. Now Asians, maybe, I have a hard time telling apart, but I don't know many Asians," he stammered. "But I never thought angels would look like this."

Centurion Julian explained, "When angels deliver messages to the sons and daughters of Adam and Eve, they are coming from the throne room of God. Their very presence reflects the glory of God, and when people see angels, usually all they see is His reflected glory and brilliance, so it is rare that they pick up the differences between them. Like Moses coming from the presence of God, his radiant face dazzled the children of Israel, and they begged him to wear a veil until the glory faded. Don't you think the Creator who took such joy in creating the variety of animals, plants, and landscapes can create heavenly beings with just as many unique characteristics and roles? Your eyes have adjusted here so that you can appreciate their differences and talents. Several have been stationed on guard duty for millennia in specific parts of the world and consequently picked up the language and attributes from that particular people group of the world. You remember when the two angels went to rescue Lot and his family and how they appeared as regular men from that region."

Jay nodded dumbly.

"If they had appeared as white, blue-eyed, and blonde-haired visitors, they would have stood out of place."

Jay nodded again.

They walked to stand before the first legionnaire. He wore a full samurai suit of armor, and although he was five foot six, his ornate helmet rose above Jay. He jerked a short bow to acknowledge Jay, as Jay stared fascinated by the two curved samurai swords strapped to his belt.

"Yasaka is the best swordsman on the team. He has studied the masters' fighting techniques for centuries, and he performs devastating strokes in the open field or city."

Yasaka made a small self-depreciating motion with his hand.

Then they stepped in front of a slender African lady with erect bearing carrying an assegai and diamond-shaped shield.

"Shumba Musiwa is your scout. She is the fastest on the team, can smell a demon within fifty meters, and is your best protection against ambush. Listen to her instincts."

Moving to the next young lady, Jay noticed in addition to the rapier on her hip, she had a bandolier with three small knives with one inch blades, scissors, and tweezers.

"Tempeste is part of your medical team...," the centurion started.

Jay grinned and pointed, "Are those small knives for fighting little demons?"

Tempeste whipped out the short but very sharp blade and held it under his nose. "This is a scalpel," she grated, as Jay jerked his head back.

The centurion continued, "I have no idea why she received her name, but you really don't want to irritate her. She does incredible microsurgery. If you are granted the privilege to answer a prayer for infertility like Sarah, Rachel, Rebekah, or Hannah, Tempeste can open a Fallopian tube or stimulate fimbriae to restore fertility. Also she can dissect out cancer at the cellular level."

Jay was glad to move to the next person as Tempeste continued to stare balefully at him.

The next man smelled like brine and carried a weighted net rolled up in his left hand and a trident in his right.

"Andrew, here is your aquatics specialist. For example, if you need a whale to swallow Jonah, someone to drive a hundred and fifty-three fish into the disciples' nets, or catch a fish with tax money, Andrew is the man for the job."

To prove this, Andrew gave a dolphin's chitter at Jay as he moved to the next figure.

"Raven, on the other hand, is an animal specialist. When you need to line up animals for Noah's ark, send quail to the children of Israel on an evening basis, communicate with Balaam's donkey or Elijah's crows, it requires a talented specialist like her."

Jay was fascinated by her appearance as her jet black hair was pulled back accentuating her hawk-shaped nose. Her head was a like a hatchet with either eye tracking independently like a chameleon.

He wasn't sure which one to look at, as either one kept flickering over to the side and making him very uncomfortable. Unexpectedly, she held out her hand to shake. Surprised, he responded and when he clasped her hand, he felt something click and look down to see four-inch razor-sharp claws spring out of her knuckles, a millimeter from his radial artery. He abruptly dropped her hand like a hot coal, and she chuckled a caw at him as he hurried down the line.

He was relieved the next person looked more normal, as he was a little creeped out by the last two. This man had a legionnaire's shield and short sword with a golden tattoo snaking down his right forearm. It read, "Born to Loose," and on his belt was a large key.

"Freddie is your locksmith. His talent is useful if you need to jailbreak anyone like Paul and Silas or Peter from their cells."

"Now Yuri Vladislav here is your strongman. His shield is reinforced and narrow for use as a door breaker to enter enemy strongholds. His specialty is the tabar."

Jay looked up in awe at this muscle-bound man who carried a long, single-bladed battle axe.

The next lady was petite compared to her neighbor, and her hijab didn't look like it provided much protection for her head. Her belt was filled with multiple flasks dangling off, and she was wearing a loaded backpack on top of a sheathed scimitar.

"Fatima is your medic and carries several medicines for emotional, spiritual, and physical injuries."

Jay asked Fatima, "What kind of medicines do you carry with you?"

Fatima replied, "Some are for combat injuries of the team, but for the target I have the *Balm of Gilead* and bandages saturated in the *Peace That Passes Understanding*. For more critical injuries, I carry IV bags of free radical binders, antioxidants, nitrous oxide, and DNA peptidase to repair mutational damage."

Jay nodded as though he had a clue to what she was talking about.

"Hong Jiantou is a talented archer whose composite bow has a greater range than the enemy's crossbows. He is ambidextrous so he can shoot with either hand, which is great when one is battling in a city and needing to take out an enemy without showing one's self."

The Asian man with his short bow, quiver full of arrows, and dagger stared at Jay solemnly.

"And finally, Ferdinand whose two-man shield is used to protect the target from the fiery arrows and sword thrusts of the enemy. He is critical in getting a person in and out under hostile fire."

Ferdinand raised his short wide legionnaire's sword and thumped his double wide shield on the ground in acknowledgment.

Briskly, the centurion turned and headed back to her console with Jay, trying to nod good-bye to the group.

"Now that you have met the team, it will be easier to understand the console," she said over her shoulder.

They walked back to her aisle of computers, and she explained, "Our legion is assigned to the Dawn Patrol. We are a rapid reactionary force who respond to the Father's commands in answer to the multitude of prayers which rise up in the morning as people take time to communicate with their Father. We are also a supplemental defensive force to those angels who are on individual guard duty for the children of God in the event of an emergency. Our role is also as pararescuers to assist the Holy Spirit in finding and saving lost children from the darkness."

Since Jay looked a little overwhelmed, she asked, "Do you know what a pararescuer does?"

Jay nodded. "An elite Air Force unit who jumps into hostile territory to help downed and injured personnel."

Satisfied Julian nodded. "As pararescuers, we are going in for the Paraclete."

She looked to see if he had caught the pun, which he hadn't. "You know, 'Paraclete' is another name for the Holy Spirit. Also as an offensive force, we establish beachheads to advance God's kingdom against the enemy."

She sat him down at the empty console next to her double wide and opened up her left screen, which showed the world globe split down the middle into dark and light. She handed him a stylus and nodded at him to tap his screen. He did, and it reproduced her screen.

"For beginners, I recommend a split screen with the upper half the globe and the lower half your visualization of the designated site," as she showed him how to shrink the globe to half its size by punching the stylus toward the screen an inch.

"You don't have to touch the screen, the stylus has sensors, which allow you to move in 3-D. For example, just point at the globe and twitch right, and the globe will move about thirty degrees east into the sunlight. Twitch left, and it moves thirty degrees west into the night. You can spin it three hundred sixty degrees and also move down to pull the north down or move up for the south. Try it."

Jay did and marveled with what ease the world spun. Centurion Julian pointed to the upper left of the screen and indicated he dip his stylus toward it. When he did, the globe reset to the slowly progressing dawn.

Centurion Julian explained, "Since we are the Dawn Patrol, our default time zone is the area fifteen degrees on either side of the sunrise. We can work in other areas, but this is our primary focus."

Jay noticed several sites in West Africa, Portugal, Spain, and the United Kingdom that had multiple red beacons indicating people praying.

"Are those churches that people are attending today?"

The centurion clicked on her screen and said, "I am designating a target for you."

Immediately, a blinking red box sprang up around one of the beacons and a tag stating Nalerigu, Ghana, appeared.

"Now, Jay, do you see that red box?"

He nodded. She sighed.

"Even though we are sitting side by side, I need you to get in the habit of closed loop communication. Just like the army when I tell you something I need you to speak into your unidirectional microphone in front of you, and this lets me know you understand what I just told you."

Jay replied, "Yes, I see the red box," as he searched for the microphone in front of him.

"You won't see the microphone. It's built into the screen. Now dip your stylus at the box on the globe."

Jay tried futilely several times until Sister Julian looked over and muttered, "Beginners."

She showed him how to click the back of the stylus so a small laser cursor appeared on his globe, and this made it much easier to aim at the box. When he dipped it once, the box jumped a hundred times and magnified across the lower half of the screen. She nodded for him to dip it again. As the magnification increased, Jay could see an image of a hospital and then multiple red hits from a small chapel, several beds, and the operating room as a surgeon and nurses bowed in prayer before a case.

The centurion handed him two ear pieces. "Are you right or left ear dominate?"

"No idea, I am left-handed," Jay offered.

"I play sports with my right hand but write with my left. I am ambi-clumsy," he joked.

She looked at him deadpan. "I will set your left earpiece to the real world and your right to the blinded world. You can hear the spiritual world and your team through the left ear and the blinkered world through the right. It's difficult at first, but you are supposed to be good at multitasking."

Immediately, dozens of petitions for healing, recovery, strength to operate, peace, and thanks for healing rang up from the hospital in his left ear.

"There are more heartfelt prayers from this hospital than from most churches on Sunday. When people are hurting, they turn to the Great Physician, the only one who can heal them. When they are financially blessed, many times they are too comfortable and do not give credit to their Creator. Although it's difficult to live with pain from illness, I've noticed that this is the time when many people are the most verbal with their Heavenly Father," Sister said.

"Many cry out in anger, or frustration and bewilderment over the unexpectedness of the illness. But God can handle their honest, searing cries and is right there with them, offering hope and comfort to get through this heartache. There are a few Christians who handle sickness with the same cheerfulness that they handle the good times. Look at this guy!"

Sister Julian clicked on the ER section of the hospital, and immediately, Jay saw on his lower screen nurses and doctors running back and forth, yelling for help and medicines. They wheeled a bruised and bloody man holding his arm into the trauma bay where the curtain had been pulled to divide the room. A man struggling to breathe was on the other side. After the doctor and nurses bandaged the man and put a sling on his arm, they left him and went to another room. The bandaged man could hear the man struggling to breathe.

"What's wrong with you?" he asked his neighbor.

"My heart is bad. I can't breathe," the patient replied shortly. Belatedly, he said, "And you?"

"I was riding my bike and got run over by a truck. I think my collarbone is broken. Hey, do you mind if I pray for you?" the bicyclist asked, as he shifted to try to get more comfortable.

A grunt came over the curtain.

"Dear Lord, I am so sorry my neighbor here is struggling to breathe, and I pray that you would be with him, give the doctors wisdom, and help him to feel better soon. If he doesn't know you as Lord and Savior, I hope he will. In Jesus name, Amen."

Both lapsed into quietness, exhausted by the effort of talking.

Sister Julian said, "Did you hear that prayer? That one will be treasured. For a person to be suffering and yet to have the courage to reach out to another sufferer is pretty incredible."

"This is a good place for you to start, Jay. Did you hear that request for help? Look to the left of your upper screen. Do you see the three boxes under the reset button? Request. Praise. Intercession. Which do you think this prayer falls under?"

"Intercession," he answered.

"Correct, so click on that and what do you see?" she asked.

"Query."

"Click on it."

Jay again dipped the stylus, and immediately, his screen went green.

"Wow, wow! Did I just blow up the screen?" he yelled.

Sister Julian smiled. "No, this is good. You have just received confirmation from the Father, Son, and Holy Spirit to answer this man's prayer and are ordered to deploy your troops. Look on my right screen. Do you see these ten images?"

He nodded and noted his face was on top.

"These are my ten decurions who I designate to react to any hot spots," Sister explained.

"Why is mine on the top?"

"I put my most experienced decurions on the bottom as I don't have to interact with them as much."

"*Ouch*," thought Jay.

"Now look at your console, expand the right of your screen and you will see your team where I had my decurions. I put your team in the order you met them from top to bottom to help you remember them. Which ones would you send for this request?" Julian asked.

Jay ran his eye down the list and decided, "Tempeste."

"As a surgeon, she might be helpful for the patient with the fractured collarbone and useful for stimulating bone deposition of the osteoblasts and reabsorption of the osteoclasts, but I was primarily thinking of the patient in congestive heart failure," she replied.

"Fat-i-ma," Jay said hesitantly.

"Fa-ti-ma," the centurion corrected him. "I hope she didn't hear that. She's the best one for helping give the diuretic to reduce cardiac afterload, stimulate the pacing node of the heart, and increase surfactant production to improve gas diffusion. Anyone else?"

"Aren't those two the only medics on the team?" Jay asked.

"Yes, but..." She showed him how to divide the lower half view of the designated site into a split screen.

"Left half is your real world, right half is what you can see."

Jay noticed that the population of the hospital seemed to almost double on the left screen as now there were bright guards stationed at the entrances and doorways, but clinging to many of the patients were dark ugly beings.

Centurion Julian nodded as Jay pointed to the hideous demons with their claws sunk into some of the patients. "You see how the enemy doesn't want to give up, and his demons of despair, depression, schizophrenia, and paranoia hang on to their victims even when they come to the hospital. You will need to send an escort with Tempeste and Fatima when they are sent to do their work."

"How about Yasaka, Shumba, Andrew, Raven, Vladislav, Ferdinand, and Jiantou?"

"That's a little overkill. You need to keep some of your force with you ready at all times in case there is another emergency. There is always a little lag time in calling the team back. Which two would you send for mainly defensive purposes?" the centurion asked.

"Vladislav and Ferdinand with their shields of protection."

"Correct. You need to keep Andrew with you as the dawn will soon be crossing the Atlantic, and you may need his aquatic specialty. To send these four, just click on their images and drag the highlighted images to the designated site and click down with your stylus. They will acknowledge the command and leave from the away platform to go to the requested spot.

Jay did that and heard, "Vladislav out," "Tempeste out," "Ferdinand out," and "FA-ti-ma out."

Jay said, "She heard, didn't she?"

Sister Julian nodded her head as they watched the four troopers appear in the ER. Vladislav and Ferdinand established their shield blockade at the door, as Tempeste and Fatima went to work on their respective patients.

"You don't want to leave your reactionary force too long there in Ghana as you may need them when the dawn hits the eastern shore of the Americas. There isn't too much happening in the Atlantic right now and no major storms until we hit the Caribbean so they can probably stay for four hours," she explained.

CHAPTER 3

FIGHTING ADDICTION

Forty-five degrees west

There was a lull in the voices as the band of dawn crossed the Atlantic. As the last islands of the Hebrides were left behind, only the occasional video of a fisherman, a traveler on a plane admiring God's dawn, and crew on a container ship pulsed up to the consoles as Jay looked up and down his row. On one screen, an Icelandic villager stomped his feet as he muttered a quick request, and then on another an Inuit steamed a frosty thanksgiving from outside his lonely house.

Jay watched, fascinated by all the various people, and as the views became fewer, he was able to focus more on the individual people. Tiring of looking at the dawn on the Atlantic with so few people, he swiped the globe on his screen a couple of times to the left and looked back to see Britain, France, Portugal, and Spain, as they now lay in the full noon day heat of the sun. There he saw a band of red lights stretching from north to south and quickly blinking off and on. He pointed to these rapidly winking out lights and asked, "What do these mean as they seem to be occurring around the same time but don't last long at all?"

Sister Julian sighed. "These are lunch prayers. Many times they are perfunctory and rattled off as a repetitive formula. Occasionally, they are genuinely meant." She indicated several of those beacons as represented by strong, steady pulses. Jay had a hard time telling which countries were which without the typical country boundaries. He did note that the boot of land jutting into the Mediterranean was Italy. There were several strong clusters of bright lights that remained persistent far longer than many others. He indicated these, and his teacher clicked on several different ones showing people in cathedrals, monasteries, convents, and homes praying fervently.

"This is the Holy Hour of prayer that many observe here and across the world. In 1673, Margaret Mary Alacoque stated she saw a vision of Jesus, and He instructed her to spend an hour meditating on His suffering in the garden of Gethsemane. You remember when Jesus asked Peter, 'Could you men not keep watch with me for one hour?'[3] Because of her example, thousands of Christians worldwide faithfully spend an hour in prayer each day."

As Jay looked back at Europe slowly revolving away, he was perplexed. "How do you tell which country is which without any marked borders?"

Sister Julian looked at him in bewilderment. "Are you seriously asking if God the Father makes a distinction between people based on artificial boundaries?"

"Not when you put it that way," Jay admitted grudgingly.

He tried to justify himself. "If this is an accurate representation of the world, why are there no clouds?"

"The weather is important," Sister responded, and with a couple of waves of her stylus, she split his upper screen into two—the left showing a plain globe, but on the right a globe covered in a layer of clouds. The bright red beacons could still be seen burning clearly, but the detailed topography was now obscured by massive swirling white formations.

"We are closely monitoring the Tropical Storm Bertha," Sister Julian said, as she pointed at an ugly dark swath of clouds churning across the Caribbean.

"As you know, the brothers and sisters in southern Haiti and eastern Cuba experienced devastating losses from the hurricane recently. The suffering would have been too much if not for our

---

[3] Matthew 26:40.

rapid response teams. They saved many, and today these saints give testimony of God's Shield of Deliverance."

Jay was embarrassed that he hadn't kept up with the news from outside the USA that closely. He was also confused by the terms Sister Julian was using.

She noticed this and pointed to the far left of the room. "Have you noticed our central command center?"

Jay was surprised as he hadn't noticed this group before standing together on a raised platform just to the upper left of the ten rows of consoles that he was in the center of. The only one he recognized was Commander Stallworth. The group bore themselves with the confidence of persons who had faced battle and won.

"They look pretty tough," he admitted.

"Commander Stallworth is the commander of our legion, and he chooses how many cohorts are sent on large scale missions. If needed, multiple legions can be deployed on the command of the Lord of Hosts. Their confidence is not in their strength, but in Him alone," Centurion Julian gently corrected. "We always have personnel on the ground, but during major disasters our motto is, 'When calls for help go up, we go down.'"

"Do you remember the EF-4 tornado, which tore through Union University in Jackson, Tennessee, on February 2, 2008?"

This time, Jay knew the event and nodded.

"Although multiple buildings were destroyed and several were injured, the most common comment in the devastation was, 'I don't see how someone wasn't killed.'

"That morning, when the leadership team met in preparation to go over their plan of action for the unstable weather, the president of the university prayed a long time. Many on the faculty were fidgety, wanting to get on with the meeting and their plans. They didn't realize that what he was doing was more important than all the plans they could have made. We had an entire legion of shields on the ground that night, giving incredible protection, and God received His glory. Later, one of the vice presidents called it 'meticulous mercy.' He commented on the multiple small details—a couch was moved to support a sagging beam providing a breathing space, a candy machine blown over provided a small safe space to shelter a student. It was such a miracle that many non-Christians who helped pull survivors from the debris field had no rational answer to explain the lack of fatalities. God was mightily glorified through this event.

"Do you remember the airplane which landed with no power in the Hudson River? Yes, the pilot was good, but we had a steadying hand on the control stick and cleared the river of boats so there was room to land with no loss of life.

"Or again, what about the tornado which tore through Hattiesburg, Mississippi, leveling William Carey University? Although there were serious injuries, again miraculously no loss of life occurred in answer to all the parents' prayers for their children."

Jay nodded his understanding and pointed out a ship in mid-Atlantic that was filled with dozens of red lights, which seemed to be racing the dawn as it headed west.

"Is that a cruise ship?" he inquired.

Centurion Julian looked more closely and magnified the view.

"I didn't think it was a cruise ship as there are too many praying people on board. Passengers on cruises usually don't make it a priority to get up this early. It is the *Logos Hope* with its volunteers on mission to the Bahamas."

There were few console windows lit up with prayer warriors as the dawn plodded across the nearly empty Atlantic and approached North and South America.

"Get ready," Sister Julian warned Jay, as a trickle of Portuguese started to come in as the sun touched the protruding tip of Brazil.

"This is about to get busy, and I would recall your other four," she added.

Jay clicked on the four glowing icons of Tempeste, Vladislav, Ferdinand, and Fatima on the right of his screen and hit recall. He heard, "Roger," and shortly thereafter, he noted that they had rejoined the team to the right.

He was distracted as a torrent of Portuguese, then Spanish, English, and French flooded in the room as the coast of Brazil was bathed with the sunrise and then the eastern coast of the United States and Canada. Hundreds of bright lights burst out along these two eastern seaboards as people started their day off right by prioritizing their time and praising their Creator, Savior, and Counselor.

Jay dipped his stylus on several of the glowing red beacons and views of rooms, big and small, popped up as multiple frames, showing a variety of people—on sofas, in chairs at tables with coffee cups and opened Bibles, outside on a roof overlooking a skyline, on the beach looking east, beside harbors, and looking up at Sugarloaf Mountain at the statue of Jesus over Rio de Janeiro. Some barely looked awake, while many mothers were frantically serving up breakfast and opening quickly with a prayer. Yet others kissed their children good-bye on the way to the bus and breathed a hedge of protection on them. There were images of people waiting in traffic jams and trying to lose their poor attitudes and others praying while swaying on buses surrounded by choking diesel fumes. It was hard to get used to the two views of the same images on his screen, as one showed white guardians surrounding and protecting their charges from the evil intents of hideous dark deformed creatures. The right screen showed people oblivious to the dangers they faced daily and cluelessly unappreciative of the Father's care for them.

The population centers burned brightly and then the lights became more diffuse as the dawn worked inland. More images of people appeared, but this time they were surrounded by greenery, jungles, pine trees of the Smokey Mountains, grasslands, and pampas.

Jay noticed that as people were praying, sometimes the image of the person they were praying for became superimposed on them as they interceded by name for that person. He noticed an older lady praying for a young man.

He said, "Excuse me, Sister Julian, what is going on here?"

She leaned over and pointed out that his Intercession box was blinking.

"Dip your stylus there," she ordered.

When he did, the superimposed image of the person being prayed for moved to the right lower screen where the image of the blinded world had been.

"Once you get used to the console, you rarely need that image except to visualize what your charge is seeing," she said.

The image of a young man was accompanied by what appeared to be a rain gauge to the side with a red reservoir. This gauge was about three quarters full.

"Hey!" he said, pointing to the gauge. "What is this? It looks like the life gauge reading on my video game champion."

Centurion Julian looked shocked and appalled at the same time, and with a voice as cold as iron she said, "This is the prayer gauge for each request, which has come before the Father. Here, this mother has been praying daily for the salvation of her son for fourteen years. As you can see, it is almost full. When it is full and the time is right, the Father will order us to make a response. Roughly, the more people who are praying for this person's salvation, healing, restoration, or revival, the higher the level of prayer in the gauge.

"It is not a direct linear increase, as it ultimately depends on the Father, the Son who is interceding, and the Holy Spirit who is providing the words for the request, but there is a general correlation. I rarely see a revival break out with a low reading in the prayer gauge, but I do see many successful answers to prayers where two or three persons are gathered together in unison, lifting their voices to the Father. You will notice that if someone prays for this person briefly, there is a small rise in the prayer meter. But when a mother gets down on her knees and prays for her son, it is like someone plugged a gas pump into the prayer gauge, and you can see the level rising."

"Do you remember when the Amalekites ambushed the children of Israel, and Joshua had to fight to protect them? When Moses prayed from the mountaintop, the prayer gauge maxed out and the Israelites started winning. But when he got tired and stopped praying, the gauge dropped and the Amalekites started winning. Aaron and Hur found a rock for Moses to sit on and helped him hold up his arms so he could continue to pray for hours so they could win the battle.[4] When others come alongside in prayer, then the more prayer going up into the prayer gauge the better. This isn't a video game as real lives hang in the balance."

Humbled, Jay resolved to keep his mouth shut.

---

[4] Exodus 17:8–13.

"Do you understand that this is not exactly how prayer works?" Julian said, as she swung her arm out to encompass the room before them.

"But we are showing this to you, using a visual example, that your intelligence can comprehend."

Jay darted a glance to his left as he thought he heard someone at the console beside him mutter, "Limited as it is."

"If you had come here two thousand years ago, instead of seeing this room where people are typing at computer consoles, you would have visualized dozens of scribes at desks recording each and every prayer on scrolls with quill pens dipped in inkwells. God told Moses to write down on a scroll the Amalekite battle so people would remember the importance of prayer.[5] We do the same thing. We want you to grasp how much the Father appreciates each and every prayer. Not only are your prayers saved and valued, but the actions and answers of the Father are also recorded. Prayer is a two-way communication with the Father," Julian explained.

Jay interrupted her, "Excuse me, I can see that prayer is important now and that God values my words, but I don't understand how prayer can be a two-way connection. I've never heard God's voice."

Julian didn't seem to mind the interruption and stopped to look at Jay.

"Jay, do you have a friend who talks a lot?"

Jay nodded.

"I have one friend when we are playing online who talks constantly and won't let me get a word in. I try to warn him about going in a booby-trapped room or running out in the open, but he never listens. He is always talking or singing and doesn't pay any attention when I am trying to help him out."

"How does it make you feel?" Julian asked.

"Pretty frustrated and makes me not want to help him when he is ignoring me," Jay answered.

"And have you ever seen a couple where one person does all the talking?"

---

5   Exodus 17:14.

"Yes," Jay replied again, "at lunch time, we have a couple at our table, and the girl always dominates the conversation. She asks her boyfriend what he thinks of her dress. Then as he opens his mouth to reply tactfully, she races away on another subject. The whole meal is filled with her talking and him opening and closing his mouth without ever being able to squeeze a word in edgewise."

"Well, Jay," Julian asked, "how much time do you spend waiting to hear God's reply?"

"I'm pretty busy in the morning trying to get ready for school," Jay replied uncomfortably.

"Jay, what do you call it when you are playing on a team and one of your teammates just drops out of the game and leaves his computer?"

"AFK, Absent From Keyboard."

"How does it make you feel?" Julian queried.

"Pretty mad, especially when we are winning and need his input and help to be able to level up," Jay answered.

"Well that is what it feels like here when you don't show up each day and communicate with your Heavenly Father."

"Even if I did stop and listen, how long would it take for an answer to come back, five or ten minutes? Can you guarantee that I would hear God's voice if I took the time to wait." Jay defended himself.

Julian replied, "There is no formula that guarantees you will hear God's voice. You cannot force God into a soft drink dispensing Machine and say, 'If I pray in a certain place for a certain time frame, I will force God to answer me.' But what you do need to know as just like your friends, it is important to wait quietly for an answer instead of always requesting. When you became a Christian, God gave you the Holy Spirit, which not only sealed you as a child of God, but also is your personal Counselor. If you listen after praying, the Holy Spirit is in you to guide you. The Spirit can give you God's answer, and many times the answer comes through His Word."

Julian continued, "When you pray and ask for help with a problem, look in the Bible for the answer. Many times, what you are going through has happened in the past, and God has told others what they need to do. So many times I hear people asking for advice and point out scripture references if they would only look them up."

Jay persisted stubbornly, "But what if I have a problem or need something and it isn't in the Bible?" As Julian opened his mouth, Jay added quickly, "And I have looked for the answer thoroughly."

Julian asked Jay, "Do you remember when you studied for your driver's license test six months ago? What did the traffic signal lights mean?"

Jay glibly recited, "Red, stop. Yellow, caution. Green, go. So," Jay continued sarcastically, "are you telling me that when I close my eyes and ask God for something, I will see a red light flash 'no,' or a green 'yes'?"

"No," Julian said sternly. "But if you wait and listen, the Holy Spirit can give you a check in your spirit so you don't go running into a booby-trapped room. Or you may feel a sense of peace that yes, you should go forward with this decision you have been wrestling over. Sometimes, there is no definite answer, and like the yellow light, you need to hold up and be patient for the answer. Prayer is not like the internet where you can google a question and get the answer right away. Also, God has put Christians in your life who you can go to and ask them to pray with you about your problem. Many times, they have gone through the same issues and can give you good advice."

"But how long do I have to wait for an answer?" Jay implored.

"It varies for different requests. Some requests take years for the answers to come. As to the speed with which a prayer gauge can fill completely, just a couple of days ago, I saw one that exploded from zero to a hundred percent with just one simple word."

Waving her hand, Julian spun the globe back two revolutions and punched the hologram with her stylus, then magnified.

A picture immediately came up of a father working under his car with his ten-year-old son kneeling beside him and passing tools. Suddenly, the jack kicked out, and the car lurched down with a sickening crunch and a choked-off yell. The dad's legs kicked in spasm and then grew still. The son stood up and screamed, "Dad!"

There was no response. The child walked over to the car, put his hands under the tire rim, and strained helplessly, but it didn't budge. He cried out, "Jesus." Beside the child's image on the console, the prayer gauge filled up and blew through the top as a thunderous voice shouted, "Go."

Immediately, Jay saw Vladislav and Ferdinand arrive on the scene, along with Fatima and Tempeste. Vladislav and Ferdinand jumped into action and placed their hands on either side of the child's hands and lifted up the undercarriage—one, two inches. The mother, who had come running in response to the scream, grabbed her husband's still legs and pulled him out. Then the car dropped back down. Immediately, while the wife was holding her husband's hands, Tempeste started chest compressions, and Fatima popped an injection of epinephrine and antioxidants to scavenge the free radicals. The man gasped and took a deep breath. His wife and child cried with relief beside him.

"Wow, that was amazing!" Jay exclaimed. He watched emergency workers arrive and paramedics bundle the dad on a stretcher. The wife waved at the dropped car to the firemen as she jumped in the ambulance to go to the hospital. One fireman squatted on his haunches to get down to eye level to listen to the boy. Another firefighter, after hearing them talk, went over and unsuccessfully tried to lift the car. It didn't budge. He looked under the car to confirm there was nothing holding it up, shook his head in disbelief, and took pictures of the accident scene.

"Usually, we cannot act so openly as it reduces the faith factor. We try to be more subtle. There are times when the Father hears a beloved child cry out. Then He says, 'GO.' All rules of engagement are lifted, and we GO in His power and might to answer that child. It is a joy to participate in such a rapid response to a desperate prayer," Julian declared.

"I can see how that would fire you up. So what ticks you off?" Jay asked.

Without a moment's hesitation, Julian's fingers flew over a console, and an earlier file was pulled up from a flicker of red. It played back a student who tossed out a quick, "Help me today," over a granola bar and coffee and then ran out the door. He slung his back-pack on, locked his feet into his bicycle pedals, and dashed off. Jay saw Yasaka and Freddie hurrying beside him, Yasaka stayed with the cyclist, clearing a nail in his way and nudging him around an unseen pothole.[6] Freddie ran interference on point, slowed a pickup and later a car by adjusting the traffic lights as the cyclist recklessly ran through two red lights on the way to class. Jay wasn't sure if the video was on fast forward or if the cyclist was really sprinting that fast. His heart was pounding from the clueless student's multiple near misses and thankful when he finally arrived intact at the school's bicycle rack. As the cyclist popped his one foot out from the pedal and tried to get off his bike, the other didn't release in time, and his foot stayed trapped. In slow motion, the bicycle fell, pulling the cyclist down and causing him to fall and scrape his knee.

He yelled, "Oh, God, why don't you listen? Why do bad things always happen to me?" Yasaka and Freddie on either side of him looked at each other and shook their heads. Such blatant blasphemy caused Yasaka to look up imploringly with raised clasped fists for just one chance to correct the student's mistaken thought pattern.

"This makes me righteously angry, not out of frustration but due to his lack of respect and thankfulness to his Heavenly Father," Julian growled.

"So you don't personally feel anger or frustration at his actions?" Jay queried innocently.

"That's correct," confirmed Julian, "we obediently do our job and do not indulge in personal feelings in carrying out our duties."

"I noticed you played the bike falling over in slow motion, while the rest of the tape was on fast forward," Jay gently pointed out…

"Oh, you mean like this?" And together, they watched the ungrateful student fall over again in slow motion.

Leaving the student's image, Jay pointed to a cluster of beacons in the Southern Hemisphere over northern Brazil. There, several prayer gauges were almost full. Julian placed a square box on one prayer beacon and magnified it with her stylus. It showed a mid-

---

[6] Exodus 23:20.

dle-aged farmer with a straw hat kneeling in his field. His calloused hand crumpled a dry clod of dirt, feeling for any moisture as his field of plants drooped helplessly. His weather-beaten face looked up and he pleaded, "O Pai, Manda-nos chuva!" (Father, send us rain!)

Julian nodded. "No other group of people appreciate God's divine help like farmers. They are close to his creation daily. They work harder than any other workers—plowing, planting, weeding, and applying pesticides—but in the end, it comes down to faith in the Heavenly Father providing the rain, which the crops must receive to survive. Many of Jesus Christ's parables relate to farming because he has a cultivator's heart."

She pointed to a specialized group on the away platform. "They are the Cloud Guiders and are assigned to these farmers' earnest pleas. They have been shepherding a group of cumulonimbus clouds from the Atlantic, which will arrive over the farms in time to save those crops."

Spinning the globe back to the northern hemisphere, there was a constellation of crimson beams a little north of the Florida Panhandle. Jay noticed a beacon there, which seemed to be pulsating in sequence with several other beacons clustered around it. Jay realized this intense beacon signaled significant distress and pointed to it.

His compatriot nodded and clicked her stylus on it to magnify.

"A major confrontation is about to occur here, and many resources have been sent to this battle," Julian commented, as the Intercession icon flashed urgently.

Jay nodded sagely. "I thought that was the state of Alabama you were pointing at, it should be a great championship game—Roll Tide!"

Julian gave Jay a glacial glance. "This is a battle with eternal consequences. Here in West Alabama, more opioid prescriptions are given out per person than anywhere else in the United States at the rate of 162 per 100 people. Because of pill mill doctors interested in making money, as well as good-intentioned doctors, who have been deliberately taught by profit-making drug companies that all patients should be completely pain-free, opioids have been prescribed freely

Shumba Musiwa

in these three counties. This has crippled many people with a paralyzing drug addiction. The evil one has used this opioid epidemic to tear families apart with this unrelenting craving, and now many children are being raised by their grandparents due to their parents' addiction. This evening, there is a battle for a hardworking coal miner named Brian who injured his back, was placed on opioids, and now can't get rid of this craving despite his best attempts. He has lost his job, his wife and children, his health and friends to satisfy this compulsion. His friends and family have been passionately pleading for his rescue together, and that is why you see so many beacons resonating in sync. This is a difficult problem, and it takes much prayer and intervention to free a soul from addiction. I am designating you and your team to rescue Brian and get him inside for treatment."

Jay glanced up at his team waiting with anticipation, took a deep breath, clicked on all ten icons, and aimed them at the target. When he turned back to the screen, he noticed a small building labeled, "Restoration." It had recently been renovated with a banner outside inviting, "Join us tonight for Celebrate Recovery."

He pulled up the split screen for handicapped viewing and the other for spiritually enhanced viewing. On the right, Jay noticed cars pulling up and people getting out. A man got out with his wife, and he seemed reluctant to go in with her. "I don't need this," he whispered to her. "I can handle this."

On the left screen, Jay watched as eight dark foul beings surrounded the man and started to drag him back to the car. There was a small one on his back twisting his head back to the car.

At this point, Jay's team arrived and took a blocking stance between the group and the car. The demons hissed in fury and frustration when they saw them. Shumba sprinted around the group, and weaving and bobbing attacked them from the rear. Two demons swore in confusion as they spun around, swung their axes at her, but her shield easily deflected their overhead blows, while her assegai darted out and stabbed at their unarmored legs. Yasaka pulled his long curved samurai sword and closed with the lead demon. A flicker of light flashed as he deftly cut off the demon's sword arm and then his head, as green gore splashed out and the body dropped.

Andrew flicked out his weighted net, wrapping it around the legs of the demon in front of him, and yanked. As his opponent sprawled backwards, he rammed his trident into his neck.

The other warriors charged the couple with their unsheathed swords, and Jay saw two dark beings run away in horror with Raven in swift pursuit. However, two stubbornly stayed, with their hands hanging on tightly to the man. This complication was resolved by Vladislav and Ferdinand. Vladislav hooked the opposing demon's shield with his shield and pulled it aside so he could chop down through the demon's forearm with his heavy tabar in one smooth motion. Ferdinand bowled the last restraining demon over with his double shield and then amputated his arm with his short sword. The two frustrated rearguard demons, who couldn't hit the rapidly weaving Shumba in front of them, suddenly sprouted arrows through their necks and collapsed. Jiantou waved his bow from his perch on the top of the building.

Brian straightened up.

"I guess it can't hurt anything to listen," he said and went in with his wife.

Jay recalled Raven from her pursuit as she wanted to take down the last two demons and had everyone set up a defensive phalanx around Brian, leaving Jiantou stationed on top of the building. Vladislav took the front, and Ferdinand covered the rear with his wide shield. The couple were welcomed into the building and soon felt comfortable with the music and acceptance by the people there.

"Now comes the hard part," Julian whispered, as she intently monitored the screen. Jay was surprised as he thought prayer had just been answered by getting Brian in the building. Sister indicated the black form clinging tightly to Brian's back which hadn't moved. Jay clicked on Yasaka to indicate he should cut off the ugly hump. Julian restrained him.

"You can't just cut this addiction off. The patient himself must initiate it; otherwise, it will damage him," she explained.

Instead, she indicated Tempeste and Fatima, so he designated them to lay their hands on Brian.

All that evening, people stood up and shared their personal testimonies of how they had unsuccessfully tried to quit their addictions by themselves but only found deliverance and joy in Christ Jesus. As people admitted their failings, Brian became more attentive as he identified with their issues. The room exploded in celebration when he stood up and confessed his own inadequacy and that he needed Jesus Christ to save him.

An explosion of fireworks erupted on the map, as the prayer processing room cheered with joy.

Once Brian opened his heart to Christ and asked for help with his addiction, Tempeste was able to unsheathe her scalpels, scissors, forceps, and other instruments. Jay noticed for the first time that Brian's black backpack had multiple tentacles, reaching out of it to latch deeply into his body, with the biggest wriggling cluster going to his head and spine. Tempeste stepped up behind him as he bowed in prayer with a shiny pair of scissors in her right hand.

"Is she going to cut his hair?" Jay wondered aloud.

"Watch!"

Tempeste came up to Brian and grabbed one of the tentacles from the backpack and traced it from there, hand over hand, up toward Brian's head. She followed the tentacle and sank her hand into Brian's head.

"That is so gross," Jay protested.

"She is tracking the binding on the mu, delta, and kappa opioid receptors and trying to free up the desensitization of them," Julian explained, as though she was talking to a medical student. Jay noticed Tempeste had a rectangular metal device in her left hand and pointed to it with a raised eyebrow.

"Nerve stimulator to ensure she is cutting the right nerve," Julian explained.

Tempeste tested the nerve and nodded approvingly as she pulled up on the writhing tentacle and cut through it with the gleaming scissors. The tentacle spasmed, the sucker on the end released, and the whole black tube was thrown on the floor. Tempeste grabbed another tentacle and went to work, occasionally exchanging her scissors for a scalpel to carefully cut and excise the connected parasite from the delicate neurons. Finally, with all the connections cut, the black backpack was completely disengaged and could be slammed to the floor.

Brian had tears running down his face as his wife hugged him, and everyone celebrated.

"A child of God has been restored, but the battle isn't over," Julian said guardedly. "This is a chronic condition in which the evil one will persistently try to cause Brian to relapse. If he can get him to relapse even once, he will attack and accuse Brian that he is a failure. He will say that it is impossible for Brian to be free and will try to get him to give up. It takes much prayer, peer support, and consistent pursuit of God to resolutely fight these attacks. I hope that Brian will continue to depend on God and not his own strength, and we will be here to fight for him. You may recall your team. They did well tonight."

Jay agreed wholeheartedly with that, and his heart sang with the celebration in the processing prayer room over Brian's victory.

After this intense battle, Jay took a deep breath and looked around the room to see what had happened during this exchange. For the first time, he noticed on the right side of the room a large pipe dispensing small charcoal briquettes, clunking into a large golden bowl. Periodically, when it filled to the brim, a woman would pick it up and carry the full bowl out while an empty bowl would replace it. When she carried the most recently filled bowl by them, Jay caught a fragrance, which surprised him as he remembered charcoal being odorless. Sister Julian noticed him sniffing as the latest bowl went by.

"What do you smell?" she asked.

"Citrus," Jay replied in wonder, "almost like oranges and maybe peaches."

"Yes, fresh Florida oranges and Chilton County, Alabama peaches," Julian nodded.

"Do you know what these bowls contain?" she interrogated Jay.

"Funny-smelling charcoal?" Jay hazarded a guess.

"No, these are the prayers of the saints,[7] and we process them to be carried to the throne room of Jehovah. There, the angels and saints

---

[7] Revelation 5:8.

Andrew

burn this prayer incense so that the smoke offering rises before the Father as a fragrance. Each person's prayer has a unique flavor, and they are heavily scented from the region they are from. For example, that bowl contained prayers of saints from Alabama and Florida."

"What about this next one that just went by which smelled like suntan oil?"

Julian sniffed appreciatively. "One of my favorites—coconut and pawpaws—must be Jamaica."

"Let me show you what caused that good smell," Julian concluded, as she clicked on a red dot coming up from the island. On the console was a pastor rejoicing in God's creation, while standing waist deep and fishing in a salt water lagoon.

"Lord, this has been a great morning, and you know I don't get away very often from the church. I know I have no right to pray this in Jesus's name, but could you please let me catch a big speckled seabass?"

Julian continued, "The Father delights to hear the prayers of his children, even in the smallest of issues. Now what will you do?"

Jay tapped Query on his console over the ebony-skinned pastor, and an affirmative green immediately lit up in response.

Jay looked over at Centurion Julian as he clicked on the Andrew icon to the right. Immediately, Andrew was deployed underwater, and Jay was amazed at how smooth Andrew swam with his webbed hands and feet, as before he had only seen him fighting on land. Clutching his trident, he hovered over the bottom until he found what he was looking for in a deep hole off the sandbar and slowly stirred a long slow moving bass. The fish tried to move away to the deep water, but he skillfully corralled it toward the shallows.

Suddenly, a tempting shiny lure flew across the water and plunked down right in front of the monster bass. Immediately, he rose up out of the water with his big yellow mouth and struck that lure. For many minutes, the pastor struggled until he finally landed the huge fish. His whoop of praise reverberated through the room, bringing smiles to several faces, and Jay confirmed the Praise tab on his console.

CHAPTER 4

FIGHTING SUICIDE

One hundred five degrees west

"Here is another delightful one," Julian said, as the sunrise continued to roll across the middle of North and South America. She turned up the volume and nodded at the two-year-old on the screen. "Her first prayer," she explained.

As the sticky-faced little girl with messed-up hair bowed her head over her breakfast, she stumbled with the words, "God is great, God is good. Let us thank him for our food."

"I hear that about three million times a day, but from a toddler, praying for the first time, I really crank up the volume. Now, if it is a twelve-year-old child saying it for the thousandth time, I am afraid I record it at a much lower volume," Julian confessed, as the smell of Apple Jacks and milk filled the room.

The smell of fresh pine and snow grew as the prayer volume diminished. Fewer dots lit up the consoles because the population thinned out while the sunrise painted the sun-capped Rockies and Andes in brilliant color. Jay clicked on an icon at the edge of the Rockies, and immediately, the image of a thirteen-year-old hunter in camo came up. He was seated in a shooting blind with his rifle resting on the opening while he carefully swept the open field in front of him with binoculars. As he did, images of his family and friends scrolled along beside him as he prayed for them while quietly focusing on his surroundings.

Commander Stallworth came over from the center to talk with Centurion Julian and noticed what Jay was watching.

"Jay, what kind of weapon is that hunter using?" the commander asked.

"A rifle."

"How do you know?"

"Well, it has a long narrow barrel and a scope," Jay replied.

"What do you think he is hunting?"

"Either deer or elk I suppose."

"Why wouldn't you go deer hunting with a shotgun?" Stallworth pursued.

"It isn't accurate and wouldn't get to the deer," Jay replied, wondering where this was going.

"Jay, too often, people shoot off a shotgun of prayer when they say, 'God, bless everyone in the church and America.' Sometimes, it may be varied by, 'God, help the missionaries.' This is good but very vague and too generalized. How do people know when God answers their prayer? This hunter is only as accurate as his rifle when he calls out specific names and requests to God. This brings joy when they are distinctly answered. What does this rifle fire?"

"A bullet?" Jay answered questioningly and wondered if this was a trick question.

"Can you see the bullet when it is fired?" Stallworth persisted.

"No, it's so fast it's invisible."

"But can you see its impact?"

"Absolutely!" Jay affirmed, as he remembered the satisfaction he felt as a second-grader when he dropped his first spike buck.

"Prayer is a lot like hunting," Stallworth continued. "You can't see the prayers shot into heaven, but you can see the impact when you specifically pray by name for people to be healed, souls saved, and broken relationships reconciled. We rejoice when God answers these accurate requests."

"Jay, you mentioned his rifle had a scope. What is a scope for?"

"It improves your focus by magnifying the target," Jay replied.

"When do you use it?" Commander Stallworth asked.

"Well, anytime I go hunting animals that I need to hit from a long distance and in video games, I use it to take out an opponent at long range. There is a switch to toggle back and forth between the scope view or regular view, and it is really useful to line up the crosshairs on a target. Sometimes, in the middle of a match, if I accidentally fire without the scope and get a hit, I yell, 'No scope!' just to let my team know I got really lucky."

"Well, Jay, the Holy Spirit is a lot like your scope. When you use a scope in hunting, you have to be quiet, completely focused to sight your scope in on a target. The same with prayer. You need to have a prayer blind each morning that you can get to, to be quiet and allow the Holy Spirit to help you sight in targets that need prayer. He will bring to mind and help you to focus by name on each person who needs to be lifted up here to the prayer center. Just like you don't pull your rifle out of a case in the blind after a year of not shooting and fire at the first twelve-pointer you see and expect to hit it. Before going hunting, you take the rifle to a target range and work on getting it sighted in. In the same way, you need to get sighted in on God. Many people don't talk to God for a year, but when a major problem comes along, they make a demand and expect an immediate result. You need to get your spirit right on a daily basis with praising God for who He is, thanking Him for what He has done, and then when your aim is right, make your request."

"Jay, have you ever shot through a dirty rifle?"

"No, my dad would kill me if I didn't clean it regularly with gun oil and cloth."

"Have you ever fired looking through a smudged and dirty scope?"

"No, you can't see anything," Jay responded.

"Well, sin is just like dirt that can throw off your shooting or blind your shot. Each time before you pray, you need to confess your sins and ask for forgiveness so you can fire accurately."

"I didn't realize prayer was so complicated. It's worse than hunting," Jay complained.

Stallworth laughed.

"Yes, it is. But ultimately so much more satisfying as you impact your targets for eternity."

Soon, the volume of praise and petition in Spanish and English picked back up as the dawn crested the West Coast of both continents, and many people woke up to start their long commute to work.

"Oh, this is bad," Centurion Julian said, as an urgent flashing beacon sprang up as a mother knelt praying for her son. Jay clicked on his superimposed image that she had brought up and enlarged it on his screen. There he saw a disheveled young man, surrounded by empty beer cans and bottles, reaching under his bed to pull out a revolver.

"He's lost his job, his girlfriend, and now he's listening to the lies being shouted at him," Julian said.

Jay noticed several foul demons filling the room hissing, "You're no good. You're a loser. Just end it all. Everyone would be better off without you. Stop the pain."

The young man with a broken spirit picked up a bullet and weighed it in his hand.

Jay quickly hit Query, even though the prayer gauge wasn't completely full. As soon as the affirmative green lit up his screen, he hit All on the right, and all ten legionnaires deployed. Since it was an emergency, he didn't have time to plan and directed five to the front and five to the back of the house.

There was a black door on both sides of the house blocking his team that he hadn't seen before on the blinded right side of the screen.

"Vladislav and Ferdinand, take down the doors," Jay said.

They nodded as they dropped their shields and slammed the doors with them. Vladislav led the assault on the front door with Yasaka, Shumba, Tempeste, and Andrew, while Ferdinand pounded on the back door with Raven, Freddie, Fatima, and Jiantou. Vladislav broke through on the second hit, swinging the door open as Shumba and Yasaka entered taking the right and the left.

Ferdinand seemed to be struggling at the back with the stubborn door.

"Should I get Freddie up to pick the lock?" Jay asked.

"No time," counseled Centurion Julian. "Look your team is in, watch out!"

Ferdinand finally broke the door open, and Raven and Freddie jumped in to the right and left respectively.

Instantly, pandemonium erupted in Jay's left ear with shrieks of anger and hatred as the demons swarmed over those who were trying to rescue their prey.

In the front room, Yasaka was a blur, slashing with his samurai sword and jumping from side to side, amputating arms, decapitating foul figures in gouts of green, and disemboweling them. His beautiful suit of armor became stained with green as he tried to clear the living room. Shumba was stabbing and thrusting with her assegai and causing curses and shrieks while taking most of the hits on her diamond shield. Suddenly, a large demon came plunging down the stairs carrying a meat hook and smashed it into her shield. He ripped it off as her left arm snapped and fell helplessly by her side. She got one good stab at the demon's gut with her assegai, but then he grabbed it, and she couldn't budge it. Before she could move, she was overwhelmed as one demon scythed her legs out from under her, and two large demons jumped on her with a mace and dagger.

Jay couldn't see her under the flaying bodies, but there was a chime, and her lighted icon went out on the side screen.

"What happened to her? Is she dead?" he helplessly asked Centurion Julian.

"No!" the centurion answered him. "Angels and demons are eternal created beings, but in a battle they can take such damage they must retire from the fight and regroup at their respective home base. You've lost one member of your squad, pay attention or you will lose the battle, and even worse this man's soul."

"Pay attention! How?" wondered Jay, as he looked at the sprawling chaos on his screen.

Vladislav dropped his shield with a roar and charged into the room. He swung his heavy tabar with one-handed ease, splitting the helmet and the skull beneath it of one of the demons on Shumba. Pulling the single blade of the battle axe out, he smashed the head of the other in with the blunt side. He whipped the axe around and decapitated the demon impaled on the assegai. Then he shifted to a two-handed grip and with a mighty yell, split the demon with the scythe from the top of his head through his torso. Andrew and Tempeste surged into the living room to form a semicircle. Andrew threw his weighted net over a demon's shield. As he tried to disentangle the net from his head, Andrew stabbed his legs out from under him and spiked his abdomen with his trident. Tempeste had her rapier out and feinted at a demon's eyes. He threw his short shield up, and she crouched down to the floor and with great finesse stabbed his Achilles tendon on his right foot. He crumpled to his right knee and when he tried to push off to take a step, dropped his shield enough so she punctured the right side of his neck with surgical precision, cutting his brachial plexus. He stared dumbfounded as his right hand dropped his sword. Then she neatly thrust into his left carotid, which started spraying green. Yasaka finished the last demon in the living room and yelled, "Clear."

"Vladislav, the stairs!" Jay yelled.

He nodded and advanced on the demons blocking their way, slashing from side to side with the tabar using his two-handed stance. Tempeste and Andrew came up behind him, while Yasaka brought up the rear as even now wounded demons rose from the floor and tried to impede their progress.

Jay realized he had been distracted and looked at the back door. Here, the second squad had run into trouble. It seemed they had stirred up an anthill of demons. Freddie's icon was only showing half its power as he was losing liquid light from his right shoulder where an axe head had broken off. He had transferred his sword to his left hand but didn't have the same strength. Raven was a raging lioness; her sword had snapped, but her extended claws were covered in green gore. As Jay watched, he saw her spring at another demon, rip his shield down, and slash his throat. Fatima, with her scimitar whirling, helped Raven cover the back entrance, while Ferdinand had gotten inside and barricaded one entrance to the kitchen with his double wide shield. Jiantou was standing on a countertop and firing a barrage of arrows over Ferdinand's shield, dropping demons in the doorway. But there were just too many demons hurling themselves suicidally at them.

"I need to tell them to fall back. They're outnumbered and can't go forward," Jay told Centurion Julian.

She shook her head no.

"But they are pinned down, taking casualties and are about to be overwhelmed," he protested.

"Yes, but they are distracting a significant number from the front of the house," Julian pointed out.

Jay glanced at that screen and saw that Vladislav was making progress. He had cleared the first landing! Even though there were demons on the second flight, they had stopped pouring down like a waterfall as Vladislav was a solid rock in the stream. He advanced but so slowly, chopping a path up the steps. Jay toggled back to the room as everything seemed to be taking so long. He saw the young man break the revolver open and put the bullet in the cylinder.

"Hurry!" he begged them.

Vladislav was halfway up the second flight when a huge troll demon jumped over the bannister onto his back and flipped them both off the stairs into the darkness below. His icon chimed and went blank. Yasaka hurried to the front, his sword hissing through the air and cutting strategically at shoulder and knee joints. Andrew took up the rear guard, swinging his heavy net at those trying to come up behind them.

Ferdinand, in response to Jay's exhortation, tried to push forward with his shield into the press of demons, but one behind the doorframe took him down from his blindside before Jiantou could cover him. When he went down, there was a rush of demons into the kitchen, and Freddie fell before them. Jay heard another two chimes as their icons blinked out. Jiantou dropped his bow as it was useless in such close quarters, drew his dagger, and went back to back with Fatima who slashed with pinpoint accuracy at demon eyes and wrists with her scimitar. Raven tore into the oncoming horde with flashing claws and slowed them down. She took three down before they took her, and there was another chime.

The young man closed the cylinder up.

Tempeste

Yasaka gained the top of the stairs and burst through the door where the young man was located, only to be met by two demons with crossbows. They fired their poisoned bolts at point blank range, and the quarrels tore through even his thick armor so that he was bleeding light. He staggered back, drew his second sword, and with a sword in each hand, simultaneously decapitated both, one on his right and the other on his left. He flew like a whirlwind into the room full of demons with both swords flashing.

Jay heard Commander Julian whisper her admiration, "Musashi technique," as he demolished half the demons before collapsing under a crush as his vitality drained from him. Andrew spun his trident using both the tines and the butt end to deadly effect, as he and Tempeste stabbed their way to the young man.

The depressed man spun the cylinder, but Tempeste slammed a scalpel into the chamber to stop its malignant spin. He raised the gun to his temple, but there was only a click as there was no bullet under the hammer. Andrew went down when a mace-welding demon hit him from behind and then smashed Tempeste's right arm.

Unhindered this time, the young man spun the chamber again, and Jay could hear the roar of approval from the demons when the bullet rotated under the hammer.

On his screen, he could see the mother praying earnestly and the prayer gauge filled, but there was nothing he could do until he saw the words on the screen, "Radio."

"Radio!" he shouted at Tempeste, and she stopped trying to fight her way back to the man but spun unhesitatingly and threw her second scalpel at the On button of a radio. It inexplicably burst into song as his trigger finger was blanching with pressure.

"Jesus loves me this I know," came bursting into song, and the demons howled in horror, recoiling away as they put their hands over their ears at the dreaded name. The name of the One who had defeated them on the cross stunned them into immobility. The victim stopped in surprise and shock as an almost forgotten song teased faint memories of an earlier time. Tempeste, with this respite, immediately gently pushed the gun down and then started massaging his forehead with her one hand. She was able to push further in as the song continued and started connecting frayed neurosynapses back together, which had been burned out by alcohol.

Over the airwaves, a teacher asked a question, "Do you feel hopeless? Do you feel like no one loves you?"

In surprise, the young man nodded.

"Jesus loves you, and He always will. No matter what you have done, you can come back to Jesus who loves you and gave His life for you."

The demons howled in agony each time the name of Jesus was mentioned. Tempeste worked furiously, limited by just one hand, but the demons were fleeing the house and their victim, so she was able to link damaged neural synapses, get acetylcholine jumping the gaps again, and accessing lost memories of the young man. He remembered the love of his mother and how she had taken him to church years before.

With the abandonment of the house, Fatima and Jiantou were able to join Tempeste on the second floor. Fatima popped him with a syringe that restored the young man's depleted endorphins and serotonin. He noticed the gun in his hand and threw it away in disgust.

Back at his console, Jay turned and saw the other seven of his squad members hovering behind him, watching the screen intently. He apologized, "Guys, I'm sorry I got you killed back there in the house. Jiantou, I probably should have placed you outside for covering fire. Ferdinand and Vladislav, I'm sorry I told you to hurry up recklessly when you were doing the right thing. Shumba, I shouldn't have sent you into an unknown room as you aren't armored."

Commander Julian spoke up, "The child is rescued, and that is all that matters. One who was lost is on the path back home. As far as placing Jiantou outside, you are right that would usually be best, but you didn't know the windows were blockaded in an identical manner to the doors, so he couldn't shoot through them anyway. Shumba, Ferdinand, and Vladislav all know the risks involved in rescuing a Child of God, but they would do it all over again."

All seven nodded in affirmation.

Jay was shaken by their dedication and overwhelmed by their forgiveness.

"What happens if I don't have what it takes to be a decurion?" he asked.

"Don't worry, you will wake up and not remember any of this," Julian reassured him.

He shook his head and tried to focus where on the globe the dawn was progressing. The smell of salt spray filled the room as the edge of light moved inexorably to the Pacific Ocean. Soon, Alaska had the morning points of prayer popping up on the consoles.

The dawn continued to march across the ocean waves until it reached one of the islands in the Pacific. There, many prayer beacons were going straight up, but there was one that looked like it was going up and splattering back down. Jay wondered why it looked like a volcano going off and nodded at it. Julian sighed sadly and reluctantly highlighted it.

"What is going on?" Jay asked, as he looked at a man sitting at a table with his head bowed. "The red beacon goes up about two stories and then splatters against an invisible barrier."

"That man recently left his wife for another woman. He is living with her and doesn't understand that unconfessed sin has broken his communication with God. Until he confesses his sin and repents, his prayer line has been disconnected, and his prayer is blocked. The only cry that will get through and restore his relationship is a 911 call of true repentance for his sin. Even then he will have to live with the results of what he had done," Julian explained.

CHAPTER 5

THE TAKEDOWN

One hundred twenty degrees east

As the dawn marched almost across the Pacific, Julian said, "Get ready for this!"

"Why?" Jay inquired.

He noticed that even though the band of light hadn't reached land in Northeast Asia, already dozens of bright red lights were suddenly springing up out of the dark in a dense concentration there and along the coast.

Sister Julian smiled again.

"We are approaching Korea, Japan, and the east coast of China. It always gets wonderfully loud and exciting every day at this time. This is the most people we will ever have praying at one time. It is an especially joyful time of pandemonium and praise."

Immediately, the consoles lit up with hundreds of people singing and praising the Lord God Almighty in Korean, Mandarin, Cantonese, Japanese, and Hakka. The consoles were being worked furiously to deal with the multitude of praise and thanksgiving pouring in like a cascade. The inboxes kept filling up faster than they could be emptied as every prayer was recorded. Jay was puzzled as he visualized many people on the screens in multiple locations tapping their fingers together and whispering. Yet when their icons were brought up, praise blared out like a loudspeaker, and he could hear clapping. He pointed this out and Julian nodded.

"In this region of the world, they cannot speak out loud because if they do, their neighbors will hear and turn them in to the internal security bureau. One day, when we all come together, they will be able to shout as loudly as their brothers and sisters in the neighboring country. Until then, it is the Father's command to magnify the volume of their worship, so it is just as if they are shouting and clapping their hands here in heaven."

On one screen, an elderly Japanese lady knelt on her traditional tatami floor with her face down, but her faithful prayers rose to heaven. Immediately, Jay could smell cypress and cedar, along with the smell of her rice straw floor that her knees and face were pressing against.

Another beacon he clicked showed Korean saints praising God with their hands lifted and a fragrance of cumin, peppers, freshly cooked rice, kimchee, and steaming green tea filled the room.

Jay noticed several throbbing beacons, which didn't seem to ever go out. He mentioned to his guide, "You know, before the dawn ever arrived at the Korean Peninsula, I saw these particular beacons burning through the night. They didn't go out then, and they still haven't gone out. They seem to be casting a brighter glow and radiate further than other sites."

Sister Julian nodded in affirmation. "These dynamos don't go out. They are churches who take the command of Nehemiah seriously to always have a watchman on the walls. Their prayer rooms are staffed twenty-four seven by volunteers who pray unceasingly for family, friends, country, and the world. This is one of the critical reasons that they send out more missionaries per capita than any other region."

"Can we see one of these churches more closely?" Jay asked.

"Let's look at Pusan," his guide agreed and magnified down to that city. There were several nonstop prayer teams in the city so they selected one at random and honed in. Jay noticed that this prayer beacon not only had straight red lines going up, but also had multiple red lines arching up and falling back to earth like a rocket that couldn't reach liftoff.

He traced out these red arcs, which fanned out in a circle like a flower from the straight lines going up. "Why do these not go up?"

"The straight lines are praise and thanksgiving going directly up to the throne room. The arching lines are petitions from the target designator."

Since Jay looked puzzled, his guide magnified down to the small prayer room. There a young man was on his knees, scrolling through his cellphone containing hundreds of names that he was specifically praying over out loud.

"This request file is updated each week with critical needs, and they are highlighted and prioritized for the prayer volunteers," Sister Julian continued, as Jay's Intercession button kept lighting up for processing and storage.

"Oh I get it," said Jay, as he nodded in understanding. "This guy is a forward observer, designating the prayer targets. I played this role in a game. I crept into the enemy camp and called in the GPS coordinates on the enemy stronghold back to Fire Control, and my 105 howitzers demolished the fortress. When the enemy forces came after me, I called down a curtain of fire between them and my position."

Jay continued enthusiastically, "Later, I crept into another enemy occupied territory and painted an enemy building with a laser. I held my laser on it and waited while an F-22 dropped a smart bomb above the cloud cover, which when it had dropped far enough then tracked down on my laser point and took out the building."

Julian looked dumbstruck but reluctantly nodded. "Your analogy is not far from the truth. The more precise prayer is, the better the result and having multiple prayer warriors in place 'lighting up' and interceding for targets is the more effective way."

Moving southwest on the map, Jay noticed that a prayer meter was slowly approaching the top and about to hit completion. He pointed it out, and his interpreter nodded in agreement and brought it up. It showed a young man walking into a nearly empty coffee shop. Jay looked at the left spirit world screen view. There he saw the same young man wearing his sunglasses inside and moving his head to the beat of his headphones while being surrounded by four dark demonic figures.

"His mother has been praying for him since birth these past twenty-five years, but he has resisted all instruction from her and accepted the party's premise from school indoctrination that there is no God. Today, her desperate prayers will be answered. Authorization has been granted for a takedown," Julian explained.

Jay clicked on six icons and heard Tempeste's "Oui, oui," Ferdinand's "Si, si," Freddie's "Right ho," Jiantou's "Shi de," saw Vladislav's nod, and Yasaka's "Ryokaishimashita!"

Jay looked suspiciously at Centurion Julian. "What did Yasaka say? Is he messing with me? There has got to be a shorter way to say yes in Japanese."

Julian just smiled and nodded at the screen as immediately, the away team left the platform and appeared in the coffee shop. Yasaka, Ferdinand, and Vladislav chopped down their opponents, while Jiantou shot his with a bow and then stationed himself at the door. Tempeste ripped the "Son-bans" off and stomped the headphones.

"Why did she do that?" Jay asked.

"We hate Son-bans, which prevent people from seeing the truth and BEATS—Brain Eradicators of All Thought—from blocking the Good News. Today, his eyes will be opened and his heart will hear of a loving Creator!"

Freddie left and returned back to the shop, leading a young man whose face lit up when he saw the first man.

"Ni hao, Xiao Zhang. Hao jiu bu jian." (Hello, Little Zhang. Long time, haven't seen you.)

"Shi ah, lao pengyou. Ni chi fan le ma?" (Yes, old friend. Have you eaten?)

"Hai mai chi, qing zhou." (Haven't yet, please sit down.)

It was surreal to see these two young men chatting away, while around them Yasaka, Ferdinand, and Vladislav stood at their posts. Freddie left and reprogrammed the red lights so a traffic jam developed and delayed the original person who was supposed to meet Mr. Zhang at the coffee shop. The friendship picked up where they had left off at high school. The childhood friend shared how he had been afraid of death and the things in the dark he couldn't see. Mr. Zhang, despite his prior atheistic teaching, agreed that there were things he didn't understand and also feared. His friend told him about the Creator God who had made everything and wanted him to have a good life, but sin had separated him from a relationship with this God. Mr. Zhang protested that he wasn't a wicked person, but his friend showed him that even one lie or one evil thing done kept him from a Holy God. He pulled out his Bible from his backpack and showed him what it said. On the spiritual screen, Jay watched as the Word of God elongated into a fiery burning sword, which touched Mr. Zhang's heart. He became very uncomfortable as the conviction of the Holy Spirit moved him to ask God for forgiveness of his sins and pray to become his child.

Suddenly, there was a brightness filling the processing room as on the screen to the right of the globe the image of a throne room appeared.

Jesus Christ standing at the right hand of God made his appeal. "Father, I paid the price."

From the throne, the Father replied, "His sins are forgiven and forgotten. Welcome home, child!"

As Mr. Zhang raised his head with a smile, the processing room erupted into cheering celebration, high fives, fist bumps, and ululating. Intense, wonderful pandemonium filled the room.

"This is why we love to have the privilege to work this room and see the prayers of the saints come to maturity. It is good to see the Holy Spirit, Jesus Christ, and God the Father receive the glory they deserve," Sister Julian said approvingly.

As the sunrise passed over Manila, many beacons of prayer started strobing heavenward. Out of all the beacons, Jay noticed one that was flickering with machine gun like rapidity and urgency. He pointed to it questioningly, and with a nod of agreement, Julian touched the light with a wand and magnified it immediately. There was a couple kneeling by their bed in anguish with tears streaming down their faces. The husband had his arm around his pregnant wife as she rocked back and forth. There was silence only broken by a moaning from the couple. Jay waited for a translation with the subtitles, but nothing appeared on the screen. He looked for an explanation, but there wasn't one. After this, silence stretched uncomfortably for five minutes, and it seemed like the room became quieter. Suddenly, a beautiful sonorous voice came rolling into the room with such power and urgency that Jay felt pulled to understand the meaning of the words. Although he couldn't understand, he felt like someone was urgently beseeching and begging for help. He started crying and didn't know why. He glanced sideways, ashamed to be embarrassed in front of steely-eyed Sister Julian, but she seemed to be getting misty-eyed also.

"Go," reverberated through the room.

Jay looked down at his screen and saw it flashing green. He tapped it, and immediately, Fatima and Tempeste icons flashed, and they appeared beside the couple. Fatima opened a jar, and immediately, a beautiful perfume wafted under Jay's nose as Fatima anointed the couple.

"The Balm of Gilead," Julian whispered in his ear by way of explanation.

Tempeste pulled out a clear glass jar from one of the many satchels she was carrying and carefully held it up to the cheek of the crying mother to catch every drop.

"Precious are the tears of his saints," Julian whispered again.[8]

As the team continued to minister to the couple, Jay asked, "Who just spoke and what was said?"

"When the hurt is too deep to pray out loud and His children do not know what to say the Holy Spirit comes alongside them. That voice you just heard was His intercession before the Father with deep groaning and petition, which they couldn't put into words. Today, they just received word that their little baby, Maria, who is due to arrive in three months, has a trisomy genetic defect and can't be expected to live long after birth. Right now, they are too devastated to speak. The doctor advised them to get an abortion and save themselves the heartache of a birth."

"What will happen?" Jay queried.

Julian cocked her head; she listened to her earbud and then tapped the console.

---

[8] Psalm 56:8.

Fatima

The words scrolled across the screen, "My precious Maria will change more hearts and impact more lives than most people who live to be adults!"

Jay was too blown away to say anything and just stared at the screen.

Julian said, "The Father loves all the little children and wants them to be loved and protected. It grieves Him beyond words with the abortions, which are carried out daily all over the world."

Over Southeast Asia, he noticed a screen, which showed a middle-aged lady climbing up a fingerlike mountain rising up from a park in the center of a bustling city. After pointing at her, the view was magnified so Jay could see her arriving at the flattened top of one of the limestone hills where a few trees precariously clung to the hillside. Several people were already up there, and she nodded to old friends who came up there daily. There were several retirees doing tai chi, while others were doing sit-ups and chin-ups on the lower branches of the trees. Three bird cages hung in the trees containing brownish blackbirds each with a painted white eye, chirping to each other as their owners rested after carrying them to the top. There was a young man who had jogged up the five hundred steps and yelled triumphantly over the city at 6:00 a.m., which really irritated those sleeping in the apartments below. In contrast to his barking cries, an erhu player was coaxing out a mournful tune with his bow.

As the lady stood facing north, the rays of the dawn started catching the tops of the skyscrapers and then slowly worked their way down. Her fervent prayers for her family, coworkers, her local fellowship, city, county, schools, and government were visible to Jay like red ripples, moving outward like a stone dropped in the nearby lake. While watching her, Jay heard the tingling of bells and looked behind him as it sounded like the jingling door bells caused by someone opening a door into a shop. Jay wondered if someone had just walked into the room. Julian shook her head no and explained, "You remember when Aaron would walk into the Holy of Holies to intercede for the Israelites he was instructed to sew golden bells on the bottom of his tunic. His jingling walk let the others know he was still moving and making intercession for the people outside. In the same way, this same tinkling you hear is our prayer tone to let us know this saint is not making personal requests, but she is making a corporate prayer for her people and country."[9]

Lives were touched and changed from her focused prayers as she looked out over the city and particularly prayed against spiritual strongholds. The dark shadows surrounding the temples to Confucius, Buddha, and Guang-xin were penetrated by the light of the gospel as she prayed that those going there would have their eyes opened. Like a mirror, she reflected God's light that revealed just how inanimate those objects truly were. Although those statues had mouths, they would never eat the oranges and food placed in front of them. They had noses, but all those incense sticks spiking up like smoking hedgehogs could never be smelled by them. They had hands, but no matter how hard people sincerely prayed, those hands would not be raised to help them.

Just as the morning light eventually lit up the entire city, she prayed that the people there would see the light of Jesus and not live in fear and darkness. Her quiet prayers were powerful, and the demons in those temple strongholds hissed in frustration with her resounding early morning appeals, which rang out like a church bell and rocked their world. They were as helpless to her cries as those living in the apartments below who couldn't tune out the 6:00 a.m. shouts from the top of the mountain.

Julian said, "She will never know the true impact of her prayers until she reaches heaven. But an incredible harvest of souls is building up because of her faithful prayers."

---

[9] Exodus 28:34–35.

CHAPTER 6

CAPTURING THE STRONGHOLD

One hundred degrees east

As the globe continued to rotate majestically, the prayer lights noticeably decreased in number as the dawn tinted the incredible Himalayas pink but conversely became more intense.

"What is going on?" asked Jay as he pointed at the decreasing numbers of light and declining volume of prayer after the crescendo of the east coast of Asia.

"Those living on the east coast have a burden for those lost children living in the dark kingdoms of Buddhism, Hinduism, and Islam. They are crying out to God that He will bring those living in darkness into the light. Their hope is to carry the gospel west like the marching dawn in an unending wave until millions of people in these areas will know Jesus as their Lord and Savior, and new pilgrims from these kingdoms will carry the gospel on west to Jerusalem. As you can see, there are believers in all these regions, and although fewer in number, their prayers are especially cherished."

A pungent smell filled the room as prayers came in, and Jay wrinkled his nose. His companion smiled at him. "Your western nose doesn't appreciate the smell of burning dried yak dung?"

"What?" Jay choked out.

"To a Tibetan, it represents their fuel source for cooking food and boiling their salt tea for an intimate time of fellowship over supper. The Father has created all smells to His praise and glory. What He has created, He appreciates when his children enjoy it."

About the time, Jay's eyes had stopped stinging and his nose watering, another horrible smell filled the room as multiple prayer lights popped up in the south. Julian quirked an eyebrow at him and said, "The special smell of durian is also an acquired one. I have heard that Westerners feel it is a terrible smell, but if they can get past it and its ugly look, they admit that it tastes wonderful. There are signs stating it is forbidden to carry into hotels and airports, but remember the Father has created all smells. Since the Thai believers have to stand strong against persecution and their families' disapproval, their prayers are uniquely identified by this powerful fruit smell."

His stylus pointed just north of the coast of Thailand near Chachoengsao, and a mountain was magnified where intense prayer beacons were burning upwards. There were several small shelters on four stilts about three feet off the ground but only about six feet long and three feet wide near the top of the mountain.

Sister Julian explained, "These prayer huts are visited by Christians seriously petitioning the Father. There is only room for a mat to sleep on, a place for a water jug, and your Bible. This man"—Julian enlarged the view until they could see up the ladder going inside—"has been fasting for seven days and begging for the salvation of his family. It is so hard to become a Christian in Thailand where every young man is expected to go to a Buddhist monastery before he is accepted as an adult and can marry. God will honor his fervent prayer."

A red line blossomed from his prayer hut that dawn and traced north impacting at a new red beacon. Curious Jay clicked on the new startup in Bangkla.

The console showed a middle-aged lady kneeling and crying with joy as she asked Jesus Christ to be her Lord and Savior. Julian showed Jay how to scroll back on what had been previously recorded. Mrs. Samporn, a thirty-seven-year-old Thai lady, was abandoned by her truck driver husband after he gave her HIV. She had no source of income and was going to a mission clinic in Bangkla for her monthly retroviral medicines. While going to the clinic, one of the other patients introduced her to the cottage industry at the back of the hospital sewing Christmas ornaments. There were about thirty ladies who sewed soft Christmas ornaments as well as ornaments for different tourist attractions, but they would stop once a day to have a devotion. These ladies welcomed Mrs. Samporn, and she felt their concern and love as many of them had been rescued from prostitution and drug use and could identify with her sense of abandonment. Their love encouraged her to consider the love of Jesus who they said loved her so much he died to pay the penalty for all the bad things she had done and would never leave her. Because of their testimony and her nephew's fervent prayer, the Holy Spirit moved in her heart and drew her to the one true God.

All her life, she had heard that there were many gods, and she had carefully put out what little food and flowers she could get on the small simple spirit house standing on a pole in the corner of her yard to placate the spirits from bringing harm to her. Now as she walked down the steps from her wooden house on stilts, she realized she had to decide if she was going to add this new God with all her other gods on the shelf or would she serve him alone. The other ladies had told her that when she became a Christian, she needed to make a clean break and get all the other god images out of her house as well as the spirit house. She regarded the spirit house and considered all the tradition wrapped up with it in her life.

Centurion Julian grimly instructed Jay, "As hard as it was for her to decide to become a Christian, this next step is even more critical and the forces of darkness won't let her go easily. That spirit house represents the enemy stronghold in her life, and they will defend it furiously. Fighting in Thailand is hard as the enemy has had such a stronghold there for many years. Make sure you send pikes with your team."

"Pikes, why?" asked Jay as he clicked the necessary instructions to Ferdinand and Vladislav and then clicked for all ten to deploy.

Centurion Julian pointed to the spiritual screen as his team deployed behind Mrs. Samporn. Immediately, Jay saw two large elephants with red hate-filled eyes in front of the spirit house, and on each of their backs was an armored mahout holding a long metal hook. Seated behind him was another armored figure with a long spear with a single blade on the side. At their feet were a dozen demons hissing and waving their weapons. They were led by a masked, six-armed figure holding a sword in each arm.

The mahouts gouged their elephants with the hooks, and they charged the team with trumpets of rage, trying to crush these invaders.

"Scatter," Julian yelled. "You can't take them head on!"

Shumba, waving her shield and assegai, and with Raven trumpeting back and waving her sword, each charged an elephant, shouting a challenge but then swerving out wide at the last second as each elephant tried to stamp out these two infuriating gnats.

Jiantou fired an arrow quickly at each mahout, but their armor was designed to deflect anything coming up from the ground. He turned and quickly ran up the steps of the house to the second floor to clamber on the roof. Vladislav and Ferdinand tried to stick their three-meter pikes in the sides behind the front legs as the elephants stormed by, but their skin was too tough. Freddie and Fatima tried to defend Vladislav as he was vulnerable using both his hands to wield the pike, while Tempeste and Andrew turned to cover Ferdinand. It was good that they did as the rider with the long single-bladed spear swept a wicked cut at Ferdinand's head as he tried to plant the pike. Andrew was barely able to throw his heavy net in the way and pull the spear aside. He almost pulled it out of the rider's hands, but the rider twisted it free and swung around for another swipe.

Meanwhile, the six-armed figure advanced menacingly like a flashing propeller with the sun glinting off the multiple twirling blades. Yasaka smoothly slid to a stop in front of the dangerous creature and held his katana with both hands above his head. Like a striking cobra, Yasaka's blade moved in a blur, and then he was back in his stance while the creature stopped in shock, as one arm was limp and draining green. Resolutely, he came on but a little more cautious, springing forward at the last minute; there was a flash of sparks as several swords struck Yasaka's armor and the right side of his neck guard was cut loose, but another arm was incapacitated. They had to spring aside as one of the elephants came between them chasing Raven, who was growling and

Hong Jian Tou

waving her sword, striking the sensitive trunk whenever the elephant tried to grab her. Tempeste and Andrew were fighting the demons trying to take down Ferdinand by protecting his back as he chased the elephant, trying to find a way to get his pike in. Tempeste took out two demons with her flickering rapier before she was bowled over and went down. There was a ding as her icon went out. Andrew spiked a demon and continued to follow Ferdinand. At this time, two demons jumped Raven in front of the elephant. She stabbed one in the chest and ripped the throat out of the other one, but this slowed her down enough for the elephant to catch her and stomp on all three, breaking her leg. It picked her up in triumph and pain with its trunk, although she raked its trunk mightily with her claws. It vindictively lifted her up extra high to slam her down, but this allowed her to get within range of the mahout. As his eyes widened in horror from a meter away, she cut off his head just before the elephant slammed her down. Her icon went out.

Andrew, in frustration, stabbed his trident into the open mouth of the angry animal, causing it to rear higher. Ferdinand seized the chance to charge in and stab the stomach of the upright elephant and braced the butt on the ground with his foot.

"Get out!" Jay didn't realize that he was screaming this as the elephant fell forward on the pike, dying but crushing Ferdinand in the process and his icon winked out. Andrew stabbed the rider as he rolled away from the toppling mountain.

Meanwhile, Shumba was trying to keep the same thing from happening as two or three demons would rush her, and she would have to stab them with her assegai and beat them off with her shield while staying outside the range of the infuriated elephant. Jiantou continued to pick demons off from the roof while waiting on his shot. The rider finally had success and struck Freddie with his spear, seriously injuring him with light draining from his chest as he could barely move. When the rider leaned over to finish him off, Jiantou was able to shoot him in the back of the neck at the chink in his armor and struck him down. The mahout sensed the collapse of his rider and found the source of danger. He gigged the elephant with his metal hook, turning him toward the house. The elephant saw Jiantou, and although he put three arrows into his head, they only made the elephant madder. It picked Jiantou off the roof with his trunk and raised him up. Just before it threw him to the ground, Jiantou shot it in the right eye, then his icon blinked off.

Yasaka reengaged the creature that now only had four functioning arms and could only use two swords for defense instead of four, and two swords on offense. Yasaka pulled out his second smaller katana and now had a sword in either hand as he moved around it swiftly. He quickly struck it from different angles, severing two more arms until it slowed from the loss of green fluid and collapsed. Yasaka had several gouges in his armor and was also losing light when he turned to try and bring down the last elephant. He stepped up to the right blind side and struck the right front leg. The hair and tough skin barely showed a mark, even with his hardened steel.

By now, all the demons were down, but Fatima was also gone and only Vladislav, Yasaka, Shumba, and Andrew were left to take down the enraged elephant with his mahout who was swinging his metal hook and trying to drive over them.

Jay remembered something he had read about the Zulus.

"Vladislav, can you hamstring his hind legs?"

He nodded in understanding and threw his pike to Andrew, who exchanged his trident for the pike with a longer reach. While Shumba danced and ululated in front of the animal further enraging it, Vladislav ran to the right blind side in the back and unslung his tabar. Using all his strength, he drove the heavy, single-bladed axe into the right Achilles tendon of the hind quarters, and the back leg collapsed. He did it again for the left back leg, and the elephant stopped going forward. Andrew, with Yasaka's help, drove the pike behind the foreleg, and finally the demonic creature was terminated. Shumba sprang up and stabbed the mahout with her assegai as he futilely waved his hook at her.

The team looked around to make sure there were no other threats and that the yard was secured.

Mrs. Samporn seemed to shake herself as she reached a momentous decision to only worship the one true God and walked over, pushing the pole down with the spirit house on top. The entire prayer processing center erupted into cheers.

CHAPTER 7

ESTABLISHING THE BEACHHEAD

Sixty degrees east

Back at the center, the dawn moved on until it started to cross over the large peninsula jutting south from Asia. There were a number of red prayer beacons urgently flashing on. From many of the consoles, Jay was impressed with the sheer number of people praying while traveling to work. He saw a train covered with people draped dangerously on the outside and packed tightly on the inside. Inside a packed bus, someone prayed as the bus rocked dangerously down a hairpin road, honking its horn, passing and missing oncoming trucks by inches, and swerving to avoid cows who seemed to have the right of way. He saw that the protection detail was having to work really hard to keep a major accident from happening.

Jay didn't know if it was the driving on the other side of the road or the near fatal mishaps that caused him to feel nauseous as he watched the praying travelers.

He asked, "Is there a holiday or are they late for an event that causes the driver to drive so reckless?"

"No, this is the typical morning work commute," Julian replied.

"But on this bus, there is something special," she added as she clicked on two red dots that were slowly progressing up a winding road toward a high mountain. "These two Christians are going to a village in this mountain valley where they have never heard of the hope of Christ. It is dangerous, and they have several people praying for them at their home church."

Jay noted that the two red dots were energized by other red supporting lines as they moved north. "What are they going to do?"

"They are going to prayer walk around this village and prepare the way for establishing a beachhead in the spiritual battle for these peoples' souls," Julian replied.

"They have timed their visit for a market day, so even though they will stand out as strangers, it won't be quite as bad as a nonmarket day."

"What is prayer walking?" Jay wondered out loud, as he watched the two men disembark with many others, bringing their goods to market in brightly colored bags.

"They don't have their eyes closed," he critiqued, as the men walked down the busy muddy main street.

"No," Julian agreed. "That would get you run over in a heartbeat," as the men dodged motorcycles and angrily honking taxis.

"Prayer walking is not like sleep walking. It has a purpose. Do you remember when God told Abraham to walk through the length and breadth of the land that he was giving to him?[10] That is what these two men are doing. They are now walking around the perimeter of the village and staking it out for the Lord. Just like the twelve spies exploring the Promised Land or the children of Israel walking around Jericho seven times, they are claiming this village for the Lord. Watch them as they pray at the government building, bus terminal, school, the small park near a spring, and several temple shrines. Now they are looking for a person of peace, someone who will welcome them."

Jay looked at the left screen and saw dozens of dark figures in the town following the two men.

"They don't look very welcoming," he pointed out.

"No, the demons don't want anyone in their stronghold to hear the good news about Jesus Christ and bring hope to their kingdom of darkness. They don't want to lose any of their subjects," Julian agreed. "But look at how these two men came prepared. Do you see

---

[10] Genesis 13:17.

how their prayer gauges are already maxed out? So many are lifting them up in support that I actually received orders in advance of their arrival for you to deploy your team for protection."

Jay immediately clicked his stylus on All, and all ten legionnaires deployed and assembled around the two men.

Jay told Jiantou to shadow the men walking down the road by moving parallel with them on the flat rooftops and for Shumba to scout ahead, while the other eight formed a protective formation. Centurion Julian approved of this disposition.

"I have seen in some villages where a demon will provoke a resident on a rooftop to throw a cinderblock or a rock on strange visitors. This will allow Jiantou to keep that from happening and also provide covering fire if there is an attack. Shumba hates demons with a passion and has a gift for sensing an attack so it is right for her to go forward."

After the men finished their perimeter sweep, they started walking down the main street. Although they had taken care in keeping their clothing drab and unassuming, people still recognized them as strangers, staring at them suspiciously and making signs to ward them off.

The dark figures became more numerous as more people gathered on the main street, and with so many vendors set up on the sidewalks, the two men had to walk in the street like everyone else.

Suddenly, Jay heard above the babble of the animals and bartering in the market Shumba yell breathlessly, "Look out, bus. Get off the street!" A chime sounded as her icon winked out.

Jay saw Jiantou rise up and start futilely shooting fifty meters up ahead where Shumba had been attacked by a group of demons. Looking up ahead, he saw a bus with several demons riding on it, careening down the road toward the two men. They continued walking unsuspectingly in the center of the narrow street.

"Get them off the street!" Jay yelled to his squad.

Now it became apparent what had been planned as the demons surged forward and planted a row of foul smelling shields on either side of the little group to keep them pinned in place until the bus could run them down.

"There." Centurion Julian pointed to an alley to their left where a shopkeeper waved a greeting to the two men.

"Yasaka, Vladislav, smash the shields on the left!" Jay yelled, as the bus came closer.

Vladislav smashed his narrow shield hard between two interlocking shields and opened a crack just wide enough for Yasaka to detach a demon's head from his shoulders and drop his shield. Jiantou didn't need any direction but rose up from the rooftop and sent two arrows to either side of the newly created opening and dropped two demons. Even better he caused another couple of demons to raise their shields to protect them from the rain of arrows. Raven and Andrew slashed the calves of two demons and dropped them, so now there was a gap four persons wide in the shield wall. This allowed Vladislav to swing his battle axe at the second row of demons, and with Yasaka slashing, they were able to cut a path through this row also.

Like scales falling from their eyes, the two men could see the shopkeeper waving at them from the front of his shop. They waved back and started walking toward him. They never even noticed the bus with the intoxicated driver, which came barreling down the street and barely missed them by two meters. Ferdinand walked behind the two prayer walkers, keeping his shield elevated over the men from a barrage of bolts of disappointment and discouragement that frustrated demon crossbowmen fired at them from above.

About ten demons regrouped at the storefront to prevent entry into the shop. Under no circumstances did they want to allow the two men to participate of any hospitality and give them an opportunity to share with the friendly storekeeper.

Jay said, "Yasaka, Vladislav, Raven, and Andrew, can you open that doorway?"

"Roger," he heard as the four of them charged up the alley.

"Freddie, Fatima, and Tempeste, help Ferdinand hold back any pursuing demons," Jay ordered.

As the two men started toward the shop, it seemed like every demon in town came charging after them from the main street. Ferdinand's double shield protected him and the two charges, but demons kept trying to go around. Fatima's scimitar, Tempeste's rapier,

Raven

and Freddie's sword were busy darting in and out trying to keep them from getting around Ferdinand's shield.

"Jiantou, we could use some supporting fire here," Jay asked, noting they were outnumbered two to one.

"Tai mang le," Jiantou muttered. (Too busy.)

Jay paused to look up and focus on the rooftop opposite the alleyway. He could see Jiantou bobbing up, firing, and ducking back down. Then moving his firing position to another part of the roof rampart. There were three demon crossbowmen opposite Jiantou on the store rooftop. They had a slower rate of fire, but they could stand up with a loaded crossbow waiting on Jiantou while the others reloaded. Every time he popped up, they took a shot at him. He was struggling to take them down without getting hit and couldn't get any shots down the alley.

"It's vitally important that those men get inside for a cup of tea. Some people are gifted with hospitality, and they will welcome newcomers. It is important when you find a person of peace like this that you pursue that friendship. Later, they will introduce you to others, and it's a natural place to share the good news. We need to establish a safe place where we can return. If we can get in there, we can set up a beachhead beacon and have somewhere to come back to on following visits," Julian explained.

Before the visitors could reach the storekeeper, a mangy, snarling dog came rushing down the alleyway, snapping at the strangers.

"Raven?" Jay yelled.

"On it," she called back.

Immediately, she peeled off from charging the doorway and hissed like a scared cat in the dog's right ear, and he slowed to snap a quick look to the right. Raven seized this opportunity to attack a demon behind the dog who was goading the dog to attack, with his spear. She grabbed the spear with her left hand, slid her right hand down it, and clawed his right wrist, slashing the tendons so that he dropped his weapon. She finished him off by spinning his spear around and stabbing him in the neck, all the time meowing and hissing. The confused dog spun around looking for the cat and completely forgot about his attack, allowing the visitors to exchange greetings with the storekeeper.

Jay had a hard time getting his mind around the two contrasting screens. On the right screen, the storekeeper nodded to the men and calmly started the traditional lengthy greeting. On the left screen, there was total pandemonium as Yasaka, Vladislav, and Andrew hit the shield wall. The demons had barricaded the door by dropping five demons on their knees with shields and spears, while the other five held their shields over their heads and used their swords. This was difficult to penetrate as Yasaka probed the center, knocking aside the spear heads, but when he tried to get close, the second row thrust their swords at him so he had to skip back. Vladislav went to the right side, but even with his shield, he couldn't get close enough to the shield wall to hew it with his battle axe. Andrew on the far left was having a similar problem as his trident was only as long as the demons' spears so he didn't have any advantage in reach. He slung his net down low, but the demons had set their shields on the ground, and he couldn't entangle their feet.

It looked bleak as the greetings finished, and the men exchanged their name cards with each other and were about to say good-bye.

Jay heard Jiantou grunt with satisfaction. One of the crossbow-men leaned over the parapet to take a shot at Ferdinand as his front was exposed while he held the shield on his back during the greetings. Jiantou shot the crossbowman through the neck while he was leaning down and then simultaneously exchanged fire with the second cross-bowmen whose bolt grazed Jiantou's helmet, but Jiantou's arrow took him through the eye. The third crossbowman was caught with his foot holding the crossbow down while he pulled the cord back with both hands, and Jiantou's third arrow took him in the chest.

"Get me a shot," Jiantou pleaded, as he waited with a bent bow opposite the impenetrable phalanx of shields.

Raven growled with frustration and sprinted to the barri-caded window beside the obstructed door. She dropped her sword, launched herself up to the window sill, and scrabbled for a pur-chase with her claws, getting just enough to be able to swing herself over to come crashing down on the back row of upturned shields.

Her weight caused two shields to collapse, and their owners were instantly distracted as they started stabbing at Raven who slashed and bit their ankles. This totally disrupted the turtle formation as Jiantou shouted, "Yes," and shot the now exposed center spearman on the front row through the head. He dropped as did his shield. Through this gap, Yasaka held his sword upright and leaned into it as he brushed the two right spears aside and spun in close to the shield wall before unleashing his sword on the two left hapless spearman. Vladislav gave up on trying to get in on the right and followed him in and then cleaved the head of another spearman. Andrew followed right behind and flung his net over two swordsmen on the back row, entangling them like fish and then dispatching them with his trident. Yasaka finished off the distracted swordsmen on the back row, while Vladislav crushed the last spearman. They could now push their way into the store searching for any hidden demons behind the counters, but it appeared they had all guarded the front door.

As the storekeeper glanced down at both of the men's name cards, he noticed the city they were from and mentioned his niece taught at a certain high school there. One of the men replied that his child went to school there. They started chatting excitedly about the same people they knew. The storekeeper invited them in for some tea, and they gladly accepted.

Freddie, Fatima, and Tempeste followed them in, stepping over the mound of broken bodies, and Fatima rushed to Raven who was buried under the pile. Tempeste helped drag her out, and she was a horrible sight with light leaking from six wounds and green gore dripping from her claws and mouth.

"Water," she croaked, and gratefully drank, then spat out the foul-tasting bile.

Jay looked at her icon with concern as it was very faint. Using bandages from her backpack, Fatima quickly bound up the worst of her gashes. The bleeding stab wounds she plugged with a self-sealing stick that swelled on contact with the light. With a light infusion, Raven's vital light picked up and stabilized. Ferdinand wedged his shield in the door and braced it. Although the demons shrieked and beat upon it, none of them were going to be able to get in. Tempeste and Andrew monitored the doorway and the barricaded windows.

"Jay, you need to set up the beachhead beacon now," Julian told him.

Jay looked at her quizzically.

"I forgot you don't know. Once we've captured a point in the enemy stronghold and found a person of peace, it is imperative to place a beachhead beacon on top of the house and claim it. This keeps the demons at bay from the host family and allows us to be able to return to build on what was established the first time. Just let Freddie know, and he will take care of it."

Jay nodded and said, "Freddie, you can set up the beachhead beacon now."

Freddie nodded and started to leave the room where the men were ceremonially pouring the salty tea. Yasaka stopped him and took point, leading the way up the stairs to the second floor, with Vladislav dragging behind as a rearguard. After confirming the second floor was clear, they carefully went up the next flight of stairs and exited in a crouch onto the rooftop. Except for the three bodies of the crossbowmen, no-one else was up there. They could hear the shrieking and banging on the windows and door downstairs as the demons surrounded the store shop. Freddie quickly assembled the specially designed cross from his backpack. Like a lightning rod, it drew a beam of light from the heavens, which hit and then flowed protectively over the house like an upside-down, bell-shaped glass jar. The demons yelled even louder, if possible, and recoiled from the pure beautiful light encasing the house. They backed off from the house and hissed in frustration.

As the men finished their visit, their host walked them to the door. The battered team drew up in a phalanx around the two men to escort them to the bus station and keep the intimidated demons at bay. Although the visitors insisted the storekeeper return to his shop, to show how much he appreciated their visit, he walked them down the alleyway and halfway down main street.

As the men got back on the bus, a red bulls-eye's icon was left on the village, and Julian commented, "Prayers have been answered on this first exploration trip. These men arrived safely, were able to pray and met a person of peace. This task was accomplished by the supportive prayers of other Christians and two men willing to risk going to a place where they had never been before. Hopefully, when they return, they can share the good news of Jesus Christ's love and sacrifice with these villagers. Then the Holy Spirit can draw these lost children to their Heavenly Father, and we can celebrate. You know this prayer walking can be done anywhere to target an area and people for prayer. Where do you think you could prayer walk?"

Jay responded thoughtfully, "I guess walking around my school halls and church classes would be good places to start."

Julian nodded in agreement.

"You know," Jay said, "this reminds me of a video game when I am a part of a team going into an unknown castle or land, which is dark. As I go through doorways and passages, there is a map that lights up in the bottom right hand corner of my console, showing my progress and revealing any traps for the guys on my team. It stays lit where everyone can see the newly explored region. This prayer walking is similar as new prospects are revealed and newly discovered needs are relayed to Christians back at the home church."

"Now that the target has been identified, I guess we can let people know about it and call down prayers. Like an artillery forward observer, these two men have bracketed the target and now they can say, 'Fire for effect,' and hammer the target with repeated barrages of prayer."

As Central Asia came into view, suddenly a warning klaxon sounded. Jay noticed his companion urgently magnify a Middle Eastern country, then a city, then a block to focus on a small nondescript building with a small cross. On his right screen, he saw inside about twenty men on one side of the room with the women and children on the other side of the room. In addition, on the left screen were about ten military people with shields surrounding the building, invisible to all but the unseen observers. Centurion Julian said, "We have a situation here and I request permission to deploy all squads."

Jay looked up and saw Commander Stallworth at the elevated nerve center of the room. He said something, received confirmation, and nodded at Centurion Julian. Suddenly, all eleven consoles on Jay's row flashed green, and he, with all the other decurions, reflexively stabbed Deploy.

Immediately, he saw his team, along with nine others, appear on his screen and take up defensive positions around the little church. On this deployment, he saw that all ten of his members were carrying shields.

From the far side of town, an older model truck approached the center of town, and hovering over it was a black skull icon that Jay had never seen before. The truck was magnified, and like infrared vision, the inside could be seen to hold several drums of stinking fertilizer and diesel oil. The person driving it was filled with anger and rage but carefully avoided any sudden turns or stops. Surrounding him were dark figures who laughed and prodded him with swords of hatred and death. Jay looked at his fellow brothers and sisters in the church unaware of the danger approaching them. He checked, and the prayer meter was full.

He looked at Centurion Julian, "What will happen to them?"

"They are calling out to Jehovah-Nissi, Jehovah is our Banner, and just like when Moses raised his staff, we will see if Jehovah will rally his protection on them, although all seems lost. The Father knows and loves every single one of them, and He will decide how much we can intervene. This is a major decision, much too high for us," Julian replied, as she magnified a feed from the throne room.

She focused on the tallest of all the angels there standing at attention and said, "Yes!" when the angel bowed to the Father and strode out of the room. As he did, he unsheathed a huge broadsword strapped across his back.

"Who is that?" Jay whispered.

"It is a very difficult task to take the life of one of the Father's creations. This angel has been designated to do the hard jobs. Do you remember the Angel of Death in the tenth plague? He is Gideon's right hand, the guardian of the Ark of the Covenant, the Defender of the Lord's Armies, protector of Elijah, Slayer of Sennacherib's army, and Discipliner of Ananias and Sapphira. When the time of judgment arrives, he is summoned."

On the left screen, Jay saw the champion appear and take his stance in the center of the road, seventy meters from the church. He drew a line in the sand with the tip of his sword and held his sword outstretched pointing at the truck, which suddenly sped up and barreled down the road. When the tip of the sword touched the front of the truck, one of the barrels fell over, and the whole truck vaporized in a huge explosion. A blast wave rolled out from it, but the overlapping shield wall linked side by side bent slightly at the top and deflected most of the blast so only windows were shattered and the roof lifted. The structural integrity, however, was maintained and all the lives saved in the building. As the dazed worshippers stumbled out of the building, they stared at the smoking wreckage and gave God the glory for their deliverance.

In the prayer room, cheers and whoops broke out. Jay was stunned, but Julian looked somber. "It is sad to take the life of one who will never again have the chance to accept Christ for eternity. However, he made his choice to bring death, and our children must be protected."

"Sometimes, it does not end like this, and we welcome home God's sons and daughters as martyrs with celebration and rejoicing, but this day they are saved to be a testimony to those around them."

CHAPTER 8

THE BREAKOUT

Thirty degrees east

The mood was more subdued as the golden line slowly traced its way across the Red Sea and along the east coast of Africa. But then the singing started as the red lights came on as multiple dialects rolled out from the foot-tapping Swahili to the distinctive Ndebele clicks.

South of the Zambezi River, a joyful light jumped upward, and Julian clicked on it. Immediately, the smell of boiling mealie meal, milk tea, and fresh rain after nine months of the dry season filled the room. "O Mwari wakanaka," rang out with ululating whoops as the subtitle, "God is so good," translated the Shona song into English across the bottom. It was a time of thanksgiving for answered prayer as oily, grimy volunteers stood beside a drilling rig with fresh water bubbling up from the pipe. The children were dancing with joy, and the adults were singing and stamping their feet as the dust rose in a cloud of celebration.

Jay could not help but see Shumba swaying with the joyous beat as her feet unconsciously shuffled in time as she hummed the same tune. A thought crossed his mind. "Why does Shumba always take point?" he asked. "This is the most hazardous role, and of all the soldiers in my squad, she gets taken out the most frequently. It can't be a good feeling to be overwhelmed by the enemy when she discovers their ambush."

Julian nodded. "She has watched over her people for so long she feels their pain most acutely and hates the forces of darkness. She has seen the people struggle against the fear of witch doctors, the ugly death masks of malaria, HIV, starvation, malnutrition, thirst, and wars. Yet through it all, Christians have continued to praise God and rejoice in his Son Jesus Christ. The Holy Spirit enables them to dance for the Lord, even though their bellies are hungry, and they have to walk five miles home after church. Shumba, like her name, is a lioness who hunts in the darkness against the forces of evil. She is passionate about saving the children of God, and that is why she is willing to do anything to frustrate the plans of the wicked, even if it means she is defeated by the triggering of an ambush too soon if this will result in her charge to escape free."

Jay looked back at the screen. Even from this great distance, Jay could feel the infectious enthusiasm of the people.

Julian said, "This almost didn't happen. A week ago, the drilling rig was locked up in customs with red tape. To the missionary couple who had invited this group of Louisiana oil rig volunteers to give up their vacation and buy an expensive plane ticket, things seemed hopeless for using their skills. The group could only be here for two weeks, and their trip was useless without their drilling rig and pipes."

She reversed the video quickly, and the scene shifted to the couple on their knees praying for release of the rig and crying out to the Father. Jay was impressed with the intensity of their prayers, but the greed of the customs official seemed to keep the prayer meter from rising to the top. Julian said, "This missionary couple did what many missionaries do and scheduled a difficult task around their birthday. It is the wife's birthday tomorrow, so watch this."

On the next day, people from all over the world who knew this couple lifted up a special prayer for them on her birthday. Even though they knew nothing about the situation, bright red lines came from different continents to this site in Africa and then like living red yarn intertwined with the couple's beacon. It became broader, deeper, more ruby red as multiple prayers united together, and their blaze filled the room. The prayer meter blew through the top. Jay watched Freddie, Vladislav, and Shumba being deployed to the office. While

Freddie

the official was signing a multitude of forms, he became distracted when flirting with his secretary. Freddie slid the drilling rig's custom form from the stack "waiting on a bribe" to the "bribe received" stack, and the official unknowingly signed it and released the rig from customs just in time. Now the ladies were rejoicing that they wouldn't have to walk five miles each way just to get water every day. Water is so heavy, and balancing it on their head or pushing a wheelbarrow is a terribly hard task. Because of this new borehole, people now have the opportunity to hear about Jesus, the Living Water of life.

Shortly after the dawn moved past the celebration at the well, Jay saw another urgent red beacon flashing up. As he clicked on and magnified it, the scene of a dirty, hot prison cell came up. There, an elderly ebony man knelt motionless in prayer beside his mat on the floor. Dozens of people were praying for him and his unjust imprisonment for his Christian testimony. Red beacons from multiple locations were relayed toward him. Jay watched with anticipation as the prayers culminated in the prayer meter topping out, and when he clicked on Query, an immediate affirmation lit up green.

Jay looked over at his team on the away platform. Freddie waved at him excitedly, and Jay again noticed the gold reflective tattoo running down his bulging forearm. Jay craned his head sideways to read the letters. "Born to Loose."

"Initially, I thought Freddie had a bad prison tattoo," Jay said.

Julian nodded. "No, it is spelled correctly. No one is 'born to lose.' God has a special plan for everyone of His children who hear His voice. It is only the evil one who puts degrading messages in peoples' mind and tries to make them give up. But you are correct when you refer to it as a prison tattoo. This is not something you see every day. It's extremely special when the jailbreakers are deployed."

Jay noticed that Freddie had taken the large metal key off his belt and was now swinging it rather obviously around his right index finger.

"I guess I let Freddie take the lead on this patrol," Jay stated.

"Yes," Sister Julian agreed. Then she explained, "That's a 'Peter universal key.' It can unlock any door. You will also need to issue 'reconstruction shields.' These shields look like large clear plastic riot shields, but they reconstruct the view behind the person carrying the shield."

Jay ordered Freddie to lead the patrol and the team to pick up four "reconstruction shields." Once Vladislav, Shumba, and Ferdinand had traded out their shields for the clear ones, and Yasaka had picked one up, Jay hit Deploy.

On the left side screen, he watched the away team materialize at all four corners of an empty prison corridor. Four held up their shields over the security cameras located at each corner to reproduce the view of the empty hallway as Freddie led the others to a locked door. Jay was concerned that opening the door would be visible, but a third screen was tapped, and he could see a bored guard glancing at multiple monitors, which all showed no movement in the jail's corridor. Freddie approached the door still swinging his six-inch long metal key, which appeared medieval in appearance. Jay wondered how it could be of any use in opening the locked door as there was a coded key pad just to the right of the door. Taking the key like a pencil, Freddie tapped out a six-figure alphanumeric code, and the door clicked open.

The praying prisoner was puzzled by the door opening as this wasn't the mealtime and looked at it expectantly, but no one came in. Fatima and Tempeste entered and helped lift his frail, battered body. Fatima popped him with a stimulant and vitamins. Reenergized, his curiosity got the best of him so he shuffled over to the open door and stepped through it. Immediately, Vladislav and Shumba backed away from the security cameras in the front, holding up their six-foot shields, while Ferdinand and Yasaka covered the back of him as the group started down the hall. The last one out relocked the door. Freddie hurried down the hall to tap out another code to open the next door. When the prisoner saw it open, he hesitantly moved toward it, supported by Fatima and Tempeste. Like a Roman turtle of shields, they herded him down the hall through another locked door and two gates. Outside the prison gate, the newly released man walked in a dream toward the bustling crowds. It was just beginning to dawn on him that he was free, and he couldn't wait to tell his fellowship that their prayers had been answered.

With a smirk, Julian said, "I must admit I enjoy coming back to watch the guards' faces when they realize he is gone, and the surveillance videos give no indication to what just took place. When man has no explanation for an event only God can orchestrate, it forces him to reconsider his beliefs."

"It is amazing what God can accomplish when Christians are united in prayer. It's like a magnifying lens that light rays are passing through. Ordinarily, light beams passing through glass don't accomplish much, but when they are all focused together, they can be a powerful force that burns through paper."

Jay thought about this for a moment and muttered, "Old-fashioned."

"What did you say?" Sister Julian asked sharply.

Jay was startled that she had heard him. It must be her years of teaching school had sharpened her hearing.

"No one uses a magnifying glass anymore. You just click to zoom in," he explained and mimicked Julian's earlier movements with the stylus on the computer to enlarge scenes from around the globe.

Julian looked surprised and asked him, "What analogy would you use to describe prayer?"

That was tough, the ball was in Jay's court now. He looked down at the globe with the red prayer beacons, hoping for some inspiration. Then it hit him.

"Laser," he said softly. Then more confidently, he added, "Lasers!"

Sister Julian raised an eyebrow inquiringly.

"Lasers occur when the electrons of certain glasses or crystals are excited by electricity and then give off photons when they drop back to their resting state. They all have the same wavelength and are 'coherent.' The light that comes out is pure and united, unidirectional with a very tight beam and very powerful, able to cut through metal," Jay explained.

A verse returned to him, "Like a two-edged sword," he added on enthusiastically.

"Prayer is like a laser when a group of Christians come together in one accord, and all get on the same wavelength for a particular

Yuri Vladislav

petition, like a revival or illness. This allows God to pour his power out on the request," he concluded triumphantly.

"The Word of God is like a two-edged sword," his counselor gently corrected him. "But your prayer analogy with the laser is good." She nodded approvingly. "I do believe you might be teachable. Now, look to the north."

She indicated a suburb outside of Moscow where multiple prayer beacons exploded for an eighty-five-year-old grandmother located at a hospital. Jay clicked on these requests. He saw she was suffering from coronavirus and struggling to maintain her oxygen saturation on a ventilator.

"We will have an incredible celebration when she comes home, but right now she is vitally important as the central support of her fellowship, family, and community. She is a mighty prayer warrior, and the enemy wants to see her silenced using this epidemic of Covid-19," said Julian.

"She is in the ICU on a ventilator, and her condition is deteriorating while her guardian is under attack. He requests reinforcements."

Jay clicked again on another blinking icon, and on the split screen, he could see an intubated elderly patient but could also see a guardian angel in the ICU. He was backed into a corner by three hideous demons who kept stabbing at him looking for an opening, as he furiously slashed and parried. A fourth demon was adjusting dials on the ventilator and fiddling with the IV tubing. As the prayer meter maxed out and the green confirmation popped up, Jay yelled, "Vladislav, your lead. Go."

Vladislav raised his shield in acknowledgment, and immediately, the Dawn Patrol dropped into the ICU room. Vladislav was on his home field now and stormed into the group in the corner. He decapitated one demon with a mighty sweep of his axe and cleaved in the helmet of another with the back end. The third demon barely had time for a shriek of fury before Yasaka sliced him in half with his katana.

As Ferdinand dispatched the demon at the ventilator, Andrew muttered, "You didn't leave me a single one."

"You guys took your time getting here," the disheveled guard complained.

"You know, rookie decurions," Raven explained.

"Ah," said the guard knowingly and nodded his head.

Jay protested to Commander Julian, "How could I have gone any faster? I clicked Send just as soon as we were green-lighted."

Julian just nodded at him.

Meanwhile, Fatima was muttering to herself over the ventilator, "What, a tidal volume of eight hundred? She doesn't weigh over fifty kilos. Respiratory rate of twenty? This isn't jet ventilation, are they trying to blow her lungs out? Look only five of PEEP! No wonder they can't keep her alveoli open."

She turned to Tempeste who had sheathed her rapier.

"Tempeste, can you check the IV. He was messing with it when we arrived."

Tempeste nodded. "Oui, there is air in the line. I will draw it out."

"Good," replied Fatima. Taking a bag from her backpack, she handed it to Tempeste. "After you do that, can you please hang this bag of immunomodulators and see if we can stabilize her raging cytokine storm as her immune system is overreacting to the virus? There is too much inflammation building up in her lungs and other organs. She has multiple microclots and needs heparin. Also, do you mind putting some nannites in her ET tube to try and stent her alveoli open from all the fluid on board?"

Tempeste hung the bag and sprayed some nannites down the tube after disconnecting and reconnecting quickly.

"She is old but in fairly good health from all her outside activity. I think we can stabilize her and help her pull through if we can maintain here," Fatima declared.

The group standing around nodded, and the solo guard said, "Thanks, she is a treasure, and so many people depend on her for prayer and encouragement. She took care of her husband who suffered with dementia for twenty-three years and prayed for every person she knew in the community. Many came to know Christ through her love and support."

At that moment, the lights flickered out and the ventilator started beeping. The emergency lighting came on.

"Another power outage," muttered Vladislav.

"How much battery time do we have on that ventilator?" Tempeste asked.

"About thirty minutes," Fatima replied after checking quickly.

"They had better get the backup generator on line quickly," Tempeste said.

About that time, the *whump-whump-whump* of the diesel generator could be heard, and the lights brightened.

Everyone else cheered up, except Vladislav who still looked concerned.

"Request permission to scout and secure the generator, sir!" he requested.

"Why?" asked Jay.

"I know the enemy likes to strike at weak links and a lot can go wrong with a generator," he replied.

"Permission granted."

Vladislav pointed out five of the team, and leaving Tempeste, Fatima, Freddie, and Andrew behind, he headed downstairs to the basement.

Jay followed him on the split monitor while also watching the healers work on the patient. Vladislav carefully opened the door at the top of the stairs and confirmed his worst fears. Inside the basement, there were at least three platoons of demons, and the cover cap to the generator was dangling off on its chain. The large vibrating generator was shaking and jostling the diesel out on the floor. Soon, the tank would be empty, and the ventilator would die.

Vladislav gave a roar and charged down the stairs, smashing through the sentry on duty there. The demons turned to the stairs and at least twenty surged toward them, while another ten took up a defensive perimeter at the generator. Jiantou stayed at the top of the stairs and unleashed a volley of arrows at the advancing demons, dropping three before they got their shields up. Shumba and Yasaka ducked low on either side of Vladislav with his shield and swinging axe as they met the advancing group. Vladislav bashed through the first row with his shield like he was smashing a door down and chopped through the second demon, leveling him like a tree. Shumba stabbed nimbly on his left, while her shield took the blow of a mace. Yasaka pulled out his second sword as he slashed and parried at the horde, protecting the right flank. Raven and Ferdinand were able to spread out a little more on the flanks as they slashed their way off the stairwell and fought toward the generator.

Despite losing several of their own, once the element of surprise wore off, the demons formed a shield wall and slowed the small group's advance. With their spears stabbing and prodding, Vladislav couldn't reach them with his shorter axe, nor could the others break through their wall. Shumba fell when two spears lunged at her, and she could only deflect one. Yasaka's left arm was smashed with an axe when three came at him so he was down to only his right katana. Ferdinand snugged his large shield to protect the back of the group as Raven took Shumba's place. Several demons broke off and headed for the stairs with their shields up while Jiantou was running out of arrows. Meanwhile, the level of the diesel continued to drop lower as the vibrations aerosolized it and sprayed it up in the air.

The group in the ICU monitored the battle in the basement. Finally, Fatima could stand it no longer.

"Sir, requesting permission to join the battle. I cannot lose this patient."

Jay asked, "Is the patient stable enough for you to go?"

"Yes, she is, but stable or not, if the ventilator dies, so does she," Fatima answered.

Tempeste nodded in affirmation.

Jay asked, "How many do we need to leave to hold the ICU?"

"The battle is mainly in the basement, sir. I think Freddie and the guard can hold until they get back."

The guard nodded his agreement, and Freddie took up his position at the door.

"Permission granted," declared Jay.

"Finally, some action," Andrew muttered under his breath.

Fatima, Tempeste, and Andrew immediately ran down the stairs to the basement. At the cellar door, Jiantou was in desperate straits, bleeding light from his side and legs, as he was out of arrows but was furiously trying to defend the top of the stairs, stabbing with his dagger and deflecting blows with his useless bow.

"Enough for you?" he grunted at Andrew.

"Yeah," Andrew replied and launched his weighted net over Jiantou to entangle the group trying to come up. He stabbed aggressively at them with his trident as they tried to push the weighted net aside. Fatima used her height from on top of the stairwell to slash down with her scimitar on those trying to come. The scimitar, designed to be used from horseback, was effective as she split two helmets sticking up like "whack-a-mole" through the netting.

Tempeste, a little offended by such blunt force, chided, "Finesse," and expertly pithed two demons through their necks with her rapier in two darting thrusts. Andrew finished off the remaining demon and stepped over the pile on the stairs. Leaving the injured Jiantou behind, the three headed over to the battle raging just short of the generator. Surrounded by a ring of downed demons, bellowing Vladislav continued to chop with his tabar, standing back to back with Ferdinand, as by now Yasaka and Raven were down.

"Ferdinand!" Fatima yelled, as they ran to the group. He heard her, nodded, dropped down to one knee, and raised his shield over his head. She ran and jumped onto the shield, crouching down with one hand to stabilize herself. Ferdinand stood up with a mighty grunt, and she vaulted up and over to the top of the generator. On top of the generator, she hacked like a frenzied cavalryman. Using her scimitar to its full advantage, she hammered up and down, smashing the vulnerable heads below her, and the shield wall broke. Tempeste and Andrew attacked the right side of the wall and rolled it up, as the three demons there were distracted from the blows from above. The three remaining demons on the left side broke and fled.

"See," Fatima told Tempeste triumphantly, waving her scimitar from the top of the generator. "It's all about finesse."

"If that was finesse, then Ferdinand is a ballerina," Tempeste replied after using her rapier with pinpoint accuracy to finish off the last surviving demon trapped between her and Vladislav. They capped the generator after checking the level.

"One third full, good for three hours, should be enough until the blackout is fixed," Vladislav declared.

Jay gave them a thumbs-up, checked with the guardian to see that his charge was still improving, and then hit the recall.

CHAPTER 9

THE FINAL BATTLE

Five degrees east

On the central globe, the sunrise woke up those in Northern Africa and Europe; Jay realized that the dawn had progressed across all twenty-four time zones, and he was almost back to his original starting point.

Jay noticed that Sister Julian looked concerned and appeared to be in deep conversation with Commander Stallworth in front of his team. She caught his eye and jerked her head to indicate he needed to leave his console and join them.

He overheard her repeat Stallworth's question, "Is he ready?" and her reply, "Do you think it's a little early yet?"

Commander Stallworth said, "Let's see."

Centurion Julian drew her short self upright and stared intently at Jay.

"Jay, when you first arrived and met your team, you were surprised that they were not all identical."

Jay nodded slowly and a little embarrassed that she was bringing this sore point up in front of the commander.

"Now, what do you think of their differences?" she queried.

Jay looked over his team, surprised at how close he had grown to them in such a short time. Combat builds bonds that are hard to explain. He looked at Yasaka polishing his katana, Shumba rocking

KSW

Ferdinand

from foot to foot, Tempeste flipping her scalpel between her fingers, Andrew resting on his trident, Raven staring at him piercingly across her hawksbill nose, Freddie swinging his key, Yuri with his tabar, Fatima rearranging her medical kit, Jiantou checking the fletchings on the shafts of his arrows, and Ferdinand sitting on his shield nonchalantly.

"Our team couldn't fulfill the will of the Father in answering prayer if it wasn't for each person's differences and talents," Jay acknowledged.

"Whose image are you created in?" Julian hit him with another question.

"I am created in the image of God the Father," Jay replied automatically.

"What about them?" She pointed to his team, who all looked relaxed, but underneath there was an intent focus.

"Yes, each one of us is created in the image of God!" Jay declared firmly.

"Knowing that we are all created in the image of God, how does that affect the value of our cross-cultural differences?" she continued relentlessly.

There was a slight pause and then a light bulb went off in Jay's mind.

He exploded excitedly, "Wow, if I'm created in God's image and each one of you are also, then I get to know God better by getting to know each one of you better. I get to know God better by getting to know YOU and your culture better," as he stabbed a finger at Yasaka, "and I get to know God better by getting to know YOU and your culture better," as he pointed at Shumba, "and YOU and your culture," as he gestured at Fatima.

"Who am I to not want to get to know God better?" he declared.

The more he thought about it, the more excited he got. Then his expression dropped as he realized what this meant.

"Man, I wasn't going to take Spanish this semester. It's too hard. Now I guess I'll have to," he said with a sigh.

Ferdinand gave him a cherubic smile. "Si, si, Senor!" He deliberately mangled the Spanish words in a perfect imitation of Jay's slow southern drawl, and the team broke out in a laugh.

Commander Stallworth nodded and turned to Julian, "Your team is up for the next one."

Formally, she said, "Yes, sir!" She turned to Jay, motioning him toward their consoles.

For what seemed like a long time, she scrolled through several emergency events on her screen. Jay felt nervous as Commander Stallworth kept looking toward them.

Finally, Julian sighed. "Jay, there is an emergency for which I need you to deploy your team."

"Okay, where to?" he asked.

She scrolled to Nigeria where in the north was a blinking red beacon. The dawn had not yet reached it, and it was still very dark. She magnified quickly on the beacon by clicking the stylus to show a school in the mountains, which was surrounded by a few dim lights. Outside a dormitory, two trucks came to screeching halt, and the dust from the driveway rolled over them in poor light. Armed men jumped from the trucks and ran toward the front door of the dorm. Beside the men ran hissing dark figures, while others jumped up and down on the top of the trucks.

Jay queried Deploy and sent the team in after the green affirmation lit up his screen.

"Get the girls out, Jay," Sister Julian told him.

Jay said, "Vladislav and Ferdinand, block the inside of the front door with your shields. Yasaka and Shumba, hold with them. Jiantou, take the roof. Freddie, make sure the back door is unlocked. Fatima, Tempeste, Andrew, Raven, get the girls up and move them to the windows."

Like a well-disciplined troop, his team took up their positions. He looked to the left screen and saw Jiantou shooting his bow and picking the demons off the top of the two trucks. Screaming in hate, they dropped behind the men and ran with them to the door. One man smashed the door in with the butt of his AK-47. The demons shrieked with joy and slipped through the door, only to recoil at the sight of Vladislav and Ferdinand behind their shields.

Two men entered and turned on the light to the dorm. The oldest girl stood up from her bed and protectively walked forward to the door to meet them as the younger girls wailed in terror behind her.

One plucked at her as she walked by and begged her, "No, Adaeze."

Jay saw Adaeze come to a stop behind Vladislav and Ferdinand.

"What do you want?" she asked the men.

"We have come for you if you are Christians. Are you a Christian?" one of them demanded.

"Yes," she replied bravely.

One of the men flipped his bayonet up on the end of his AK-47. "Are you sure you are Christian?"

"Yes," she replied simply.

Time seemed to stand still for Jay as he frantically clicked on Request:

- Attack men?
- Apply dust and confusion?
- Loss of electricity?

But every time he clicked on Query, his screen flashed a red denial, "Stand Down."

He looked at Sister Julian. "Centurion Julian, we have to do something. He is going to kill her. What can we do?" he asked her.

She shook her head sorrowfully. "Jay, the orders we received are to stand down."

"No, no," he protested. He stood up. "Commander Stallworth, please," he yelled over to the center post.

Commander Stallworth met his gaze squarely and shook his head no.

Vladislav and Ferdinand refused to move, and the scene appeared frozen as Jay tried to think of anything he could do differently or phrase his request, but his screen still reflected back to him the words, "Stand down."

Jay turned, "Is there anything I can do to save her?"

Centurion Julian stared at him. "What else could you do?"

Haltingly, he said, "I could trade places with her."

Julian's eyes bored into his as she measured his offer and resolve. He met her gaze steadily and straightened up.

She must have found what she was looking for as she nodded approvingly. "A life must be given tonight, but it is not yours to give."

Jay turned back to the stalemate.

"Jay," she repeated as she gripped his shoulder with more strength than he could imagine in her small hand. "Look at me," she ordered. He reluctantly met her eyes.

"A good soldier must obey orders, no matter how difficult. Tell your squad to stand down!"

With a barely audible voice, Jay whispered, "Stand down."

Vladislav and Ferdinand reluctantly stepped aside. The man stepped forward and bayoneted Adaeze in the left chest, and as the blade ripped through her heart, she collapsed on the ground, dragging the AK-47 with her as she clung to the barrel.

"Now, Jay!" the centurion's shout roused him as he saw the screen flash green on the "loss of electricity" option.

"Freddie," Jay yelled.

"On it." Freddie sprinted over to the generator. It coughed once and was silent, plunging the compound into darkness.

In the pandemonium and screams in the dorm, the two men at the door couldn't advance, as the young lady had a tight grip on the AK-47, and Vladislav kicked a desk into the path of the second man. The others flung open the windows and guided the crying girls outside into the darkness. A breeze blew up blowing grit into the eyes of the men stationed by the trucks, and they couldn't see anything in the unexpected void. The girls scattered and ran up the hillsides where they could hide out until the morning light when help could arrive.

Back at the prayer processing center, Jay wiping his eyes asked, "Why?"

"She was only eighteen and had her whole life before her. She loved the Lord. Why?"

"That is the hardest question, and we don't always know the answer," Sister Julian replied. She motioned for Jay to get up and walk with her to the wall behind them. He noticed that Commander Stallworth was walking over to join them, and several others from his Legion's row joined them at the back wall. Sister Julian did something, and the wall became transparent as they crowded up to it. Jay realized that he was in a tall building overlooking a beautiful city. Just before him was a large plaza with a raised platform and a large golden throne from which a rushing stream came from. He looked down the street to the city gate and saw many people moving along the tall wall and adjoining side streets to form a vast semicircular throng before the gate.

Jay was surprised that even at this distance if he concentrated, he could clearly see individual faces and the smallest details of the incredible gates. He marveled at his eyesight after wearing glasses for so many years. The crowd, which had been chattering excitedly, dropped into a hush as an honor guard of ten people appeared in a two-row formation. Jay recognized his squad members with Shumba holding her assegai up to form an arch with Yasaka's katana. Just behind them, Vladislav held his battle axe up to touch Andrew's trident. The others had their swords up as Adaeze stepped dazedly through the open gates and walked under their arch. Her ebony face glowed with health and vitality, and she was wearing a beautiful white robe. Over her left chest was a short line of glowing golden stitching as a mark of honor. Dawning comprehension filled her eyes as she looked around.

A lady with dark ringlets stepped up to her and held out her hands. "Daughter, welcome home."

She looked at her in questioning wonder. "Granny, you don't have grey hair, and you are so much taller."

The lady in return laughed and said, "You aren't my Little One anymore either," as she gave her a hug. This signaled everyone to start cheering, ululating, and clapping their hands. Someone started humming, and immediately, "The Welcome Home" song was taken up by the voices of tens of thousands.

In the crescendo of this noise and with her relatives and friends surging around her, Adaeze shouted, "But, Granny, I want to see Jesus."

Granny beamed, nodded understandingly, and shooed a path open as she pointed up the street toward the plaza. Thanking her with a smile, Adaeze walked out the narrow opening, which gradually grew wider as everyone stepped back. Jay watched her as her walk quickened, as she looked up the street and started jogging past the people lining the street who were cheering her name. Initially, she tried to wave and bob her head in an embarrassed acknowledgment, but gradually her attention became laser focused on the plaza and the raised throne there. The cries of "Vite, vite" (quickly, quickly), "Jia You" (pour on the oil), and "Mwana, mwana" (run, run) rang out, but she tuned them out as she concentrated on pumping her arms and running up the street as fast as she could. Jay couldn't get over her speed as her robe flowed up to her knees as she sprinted at what surely must be Olympic speed up the street and maintained it for one hundred meters, then two hundred, and four hundred meters. He expected her to have to stop and catch her breath, but she kept coming.

As she approached the now packed plaza, a roar went up from thousands of voices as Jay saw a man stand up from the throne. Wearing a glittering diadem on his flowing hair and a brilliant golden robe, he stepped forward. Jay could only see his back and realized he longed to see his face. Jay was shocked to see him walk down the steps and, as if he could scarcely contain himself, run to meet the charging girl. They ran hard to each other, and when they collided, Jay was surprised they didn't knock each other over. But the king grabbed her up in a bear hug and spun her around with her feet in the air, crying, "My child, my child, welcome."

Crying, "Jesus, Jesus." She wept tears of joy on his shoulder as the crowd thundered their approval.

"Would you deny her this?" whispered Sister Julian.

"No, ma'am," he quietly replied. Looking up, he saw that his team was back and standing around.

He nodded to them and said, "Thank you very much for all you have done."

Commander Stallworth looked at Sister Julian, and she gave a small nod.

"Jay, come this way."

Commander Stallworth and Centurion Julian led the way to central command. As Jay followed them, an eerie silence fell across the prayer processing center. On his right, the large globe seemed to come to a complete halt. To his left, those decurions seated at their consoles slowly stood. The three of them stepped up the raised dais of the central command. The other commanders turned and faced them. Commander Stallworth and Centurion Julian stood in the center and faced Jay who straightened up his shoulders, conscious of his team lined up behind him.

"Jay, you have passed your final. To be able to follow orders when everything within you is shouting no was the last major requirement. You have proved your courage, resourcefulness, and sacrifice. Kneel," Commander Stallworth ordered.

Jay bent his knee and bowed his head though dazed. He heard the commander draw his sword, and a hard blow slammed his left shoulder. He hoped it was the flat side of the blade because it felt like a club had just hit him.

"Rise, Decurion!" the commander announced.

As Jay stood to his feet, he saw the entire room of decurions were on their feet and clapping. He was immediately surrounded by his team who all cheered and pounded him on his left shoulder, which just seemed accentuate the numbness there. When Ferdinand walked up to pound him, Jay was afraid he was going to end up on the floor, but Ferdinand pulled his punch. However, Raven slugged him so hard, and it stung so bad he had to look to make sure she didn't have her claws out. He could tell that she didn't mean it maliciously, though, because even though she wasn't smiling, this was the first time she looked directly at him with both eyes making contact instead of her creepy habit of both pupils wandering in different directions.

Centurion Julian said, "Jay, come here and lean over."

This time, he was conscious of the difference in his height to hers.

She stretched and raised up a shiny Roman helmet with its proud red crest signifying command and put it on his head. It felt snug but good. The weight was a little hard to get used, like wearing a football helmet in summer workouts for the first time. It also seemed to constrict his view so that it was hard to see who was pounding on his left shoulder trying to get his attention.

He turned and there was Yasaka, smiling for the first time he could remember and holding up a Roman short sword, sheathed in a hand-worked leather scabbard.

Yasaka partially slid the blade out where Jay could admire the blade.

"This steel has been refined seven times and holds a very sharp edge," Yasaka explained.

"As good as your katana?"

"No!" Yasaka bluntly stated.

"Wow, well, thank you, Yasaka."

"It's from all of us," gently corrected Tempeste, who was also smiling at him. Two people he thought he would never see smiling. Would wonders never cease?

Hong Jiantou pointed to the scabbard where three Chinese characters were burned into the leather at the top.

"Hong Jiantou" he stated as he pointed out each character.

Jay looked at the hanzi and it clicked, "Oh, it's your name."

Vladislav was right beside him, pointing out the Cyrillic script below the Chinese characters and saying his name. Jay was touched as he saw all ten names running down the length of his scabbard. He belted the scabbard on and pulled the sword in and out a couple of times to get used to the weight. It felt good to be a part of this team.

Suddenly, the globe started turning.

"Remember, Jay!" Sister Julian spoke, staring at him intently as a klaxon went off with another emergency for the Dawn Patrol.

With their yells ringing in his ears, he turned away and found that his alarm was blaring and flashing "6:10."

He realized he was back in bed as he hit his cell phone. Sitting up, he realized his left arm had gone to sleep from lying on it, and he squeezed his hand several times to get the blood flowing through it. In awe of what had just happened, he dropped to his knees beside his bed and said, "Forgive me, Father, and thank you for this experience.

May I use this memory every day to give you the praise you deserve and call out by name those who need your intervention in their lives. Help me to be a good decurion and rally prayer support for the battles, which are being fought today."

Then he quickly texted a group text, "Lunch today, we've got to talk."

His eyes fell on the Bible reading of the day:

> The Mighty One, God the LORD
> Has spoken and called the earth
> From the rising of the sun to its going down.
> Out of Zion, the perfection of beauty,
> God will shine forth.[11]

---

[11] Psalm 50:1–2.

TAKE THE PRAYER
WARRIOR CHALLENGE

I have always admired warriors. During the Vietnam War, my father was a surgeon at the 106th General Hospital in Yokohama, Japan, for three years. He would come home in the evenings telling me stories of servicemen and women whom he had taken care of, and I was fascinated by what they had experienced.

In 1972, my parents went to Rhodesia as missionaries where my father served at Sanyati Baptist Hospital for the next thirty years. During that time, I saw spiritual darkness among witch doctors who condemned my father's work at the hospital. I also saw joy and light at church celebrations when someone accepted Jesus Christ as their Lord and Savior.

Not only was there spiritual warfare, but there was also a civil war going on at this time. As a child, I noticed the war getting worse as we had to travel by convoy from Bulawayo to South Africa. Initially, the three escort pickups who accompanied the fifty-odd car convoy on the four-hour journey, each had a couple of soldiers up front and one in the back behind a .50-cal machine gun, which he spun around while sitting on a bicycle seat. Later, two shields were placed on either side of the machine gun to protect the gunner as more convoys were attacked. As it became more dangerous, revolving double-walled turrets were substituted in the back of the pickups with the now helmeted gunner having a microphone to talk to the front.

I remember how nervous I would get when driving behind the escort pickup. I would watch the machine gun turn and aim at each suspicious ambush point as we passed kopjes and clumps of mopani trees. One day, we returned from a youth retreat and were driving in the left lane as usual when the convoy was fired upon from a clump of trees. I remember the youth leaders yelling at us to get down as the entire left side of the convoy exploded in gunfire, as passengers in the vehicles returned fire with their personal weapons—FNs, G3s, Uzis, shotguns, rifles, anything to suppress fire coming from the ambush. Everyone stepped on the gas, which didn't increase the speed much in our VW van. I remember how bitterly disappointed I was as I ignored the shouted commands and raised up to look hard at the low lying scrub trees about two hundred meters away. This wasn't like any movie I had ever seen. In the movies, I could always see the people shooting or at least see smoke. Here I couldn't see the people shooting at us. There was no smoke and no tracer paths of the bullets. The bullet paths were invisible but still packed a punch when they hit. We didn't have any guns in our van so I was reassured when I heard the escort pickup come racing up on our right hand side firing in a long continuous throbbing rumble. Faster than a string of firecrackers, you couldn't pick out the sound of distinct bullets firing. It was just a loud purr of thunder with the glittering spray of spent shells shooting out into the turret. There were no casualties in that ambush, as thankfully, there were no trees or land mines across the road.

I've often wondered if prayer is a little like those invisible bullets—visually impossible to see but carry a powerful impact. During the civil war, I heard stories where prayers were miraculously answered.

One lady was hanging her washing out when she felt the need to pray. She dropped to her knees and prayed. Later, a band of guerrillas were arrested for attacking and burning the farms down on either side of hers. During their interrogation as to why the guerrillas didn't attack her farm, their leader answered the questioners.

"Where did the soldiers in white come from?"

They assured him that there weren't any soldiers, White or Black, who were with her on the farm.

But he insisted that as they assembled to attack this lone woman, she dropped to her knees. "She was surrounded by soldiers all dressed in white around her, and we were afraid."

After hearing many similar stories like this, I wondered about God's heavenly soldiers.

There were times when I questioned why God's soldiers didn't protect everyone. One night, in the summer of 1978, the guerrillas came to our mission station and bayoneted our next-door neighbor, Archie Dunaway, killing him behind the hospital while his wife Margaret was working at the hospital. When word spread that he had gone missing from the hospital, all the missionaries gathered at his house, and the national pastors came and prayed with them. Although over a dozen missionaries had been killed at other mission stations that June, the national pastors were willing to risk their lives to pray. My parents were worried that if all the missionaries were going to be killed that night, they wanted to try and save the children. My sisters were sent to be hidden at one of the national pastors' homes. He risked his family to save mine, and I will always be grateful to the Muchecheteres. The army was called to help locate Archie Dunaway and protect everyone else, but they said it was too dangerous for them to come out at night. The missionaries had to rely on God to protect them. The guerrillas didn't kill anyone else that night, and the army came the next morning to escort the missionaries off the station. But I asked myself why wasn't Archie Dunaway protected?

Later, I worked for fifteen years in several countries in East Asia. I have seen not only lost people living in fear and darkness, but also Christians living in joy despite difficult situations. I know prayer is powerful as I have seen God intervening in people's lives when they are prayed for by name.

I wrote the *Decurion* to show the power of prayer and to encourage people everywhere to take up the challenge to be warriors.

Time is gold.

It takes time to invest in a new character, buy a new skin, and upgrade a module. What you spend your time on—family, friends, or sports—shows what you value in life.

Will you take the warrior challenge to spend time in prayer each day?

THE PRAYER WARRIOR CHALLENGE

1. Monday

    Pray for your family.
    Google the GPS coordinates of your house and write them in

    _____
    Write down the names of your:
    Parents

    Siblings

    Grandparents

    Aunts and uncles

    Cousins

    Africa

    Google a country a day and pray for the people of that country with any needs they might have from the news. Cross that country out after you have prayed over it. Join hundreds of prayer warriors in the campaign to shine the light of God into each country. Pray for your brothers and sisters in Christ in each place.

    Algeria, Angola, Benin, Botswana, Burkina Faso, Burundi, Cabo Verde, Cameroon, Central African Republic, Chad, Comoros, Democratic Republic of Congo, Republic of the Congo, Côte d'Ivoire, Djibouti, Egypt, Equatorial Guinea, Eritrea, Eswatini (Swaziland), Ethiopia, Gabon, Gambia, Ghana, Guinea, Guinea-

Bissau, Kenya, Lesotho, Liberia, Libya, Madagascar, Malawi, Mali, Mauritania, Mauritius, Morocco, Mozambique, Namibia, Niger, Nigeria, Rwanda, São Tomé and Principe, Senegal, Seychelles, Sierra Leone, Somalia, South Africa, South Sudan, Sudan, Tanzania, Togo, Tunisia, Uganda, Zambia, Zimbabwe.

2. Tuesday

Pray for your church.
Google the GPS coordinates of your church and write them in here _____

Write down the names of your:
Ministers and spouses

Youth group

Those you could invite

Teachers

Ministries/outreach

Secretaries/maintenance

Europe

Google a country a day and pray for the people of that country and any needs they have, which are in the news. Cross that country out after you have prayed over it.

Albania, Andorra, Austria, Belarus, Belgium, Bosnia and Herzegovina, Bulgaria, Croatia, Cyprus, Czech Republic, Denmark, Estonia, Finland, France, Georgia, Germany, Greece, Hungary, Iceland, Ireland, Italy, Kazakhstan, Kosovo, Latvia, Liechtenstein, Lithuania, Luxembourg, Malta, Moldova, Monaco, Montenegro, Netherlands, North Macedonia, Norway,

Poland, Portugal, Romania, San Marino, Serbia, Slovakia, Slovenia, Spain, Sweden, Switzerland, Turkey, Ukraine, United Kingdom, Vatican City.

3. Wednesday

Pray for your school.
Write in the GPS coordinates _____

Pray for your classmates

Friends

Enemies

Those who need to know Christ

Teachers

Coaches

Principal

Cafeteria workers (and the food)

Maintenance/Bus drivers

Special events—start of school, games, meet you at the pole, prom, graduation

South America

    Google a country a day and pray for the people of that country and any needs they have, which are in the news. Cross that country out after you have prayed over it.

Argentina, Bolivia, Brazil, Chile, Colombia, Ecuador, French Guiana, Guyana, Paraguay, Peru, Suriname, Uruguay, Venezuela.

4. Thursday

Pray for your community.
Write the GPS coordinates here _____

Mayor

Council/aldermen

First responders
    Police
    Firemen
    Paramedics

Sanitation and maintenance

Outreach to the poor and homeless.

Mental health advocates

Addiction rehab centers

Asia

Google a country a day and pray for the people of that country and any needs they have, which are in the news. Cross that country out after you have prayed over it.

Afghanistan, Armenia, Azerbaijan, Bahrain, Bangladesh, Bhutan, Brunei, Cambodia, China, India, Indonesia, Iran, Iraq, Israel, Japan, Jordan, Kuwait, Kyrgyzstan, Laos, Lebanon, Malaysia, Maldives, Mongolia, Myanmar (Burma), Nepal, North Korea, Oman, Pakistan, Palestine, Philippines, Qatar, Russia, Saudi Arabia, Singapore, South Korea, Sri Lanka, Syria,

Taiwan, Tajikistan, Thailand, Timor-Leste, Turkmenistan, United Arab Emirates, Uzbekistan, Vietnam, Yemen.

5. Friday

Pray for your nation.
GPS coordinates of your state/province capitol_____

President/prime minister

Vice president

Senators

Congressmen and congresswomen

Governor

State representatives

Supreme Court

Military members

North America

Google a country a day and pray for the people of that country and any needs they have, which are in the news. Cross that country out after you have prayed over it.

Anguilla, Antigua and Barbuda, Bahamas, Barbados, Belize, Bermuda, British Virgin Islands, Canada, Costa Rica, Cuba, Dominica, Dominican Republic, El Salvador, Guadeloupe, Grenada, Greenland, Guatemala, Haiti, Honduras, Jamaica, Martinique, Mexico, Montserrat, Nicaragua, Netherlands Antilles—Aruba, Bonaire, Curaçao, Panama, Puerto Rico, Saint Kitts and Nevis, Saint Lucia, Saint Martin, Saint Vincent and the Grenadines, Trinidad and Tobago, Turks and Caicos Islands, United States of America, US Virgin Islands.

6. Saturday

Pray for missionaries who go out to share the Good News of Christ.

Relationships, language learning, children's education, safety and health.

Home missionaries

Chaplains

Jail outreach

Overseas missionaries

Google a country a day and pray for the people of that country and any needs they have, which are in the news. Cross that country out after you have prayed over it.

American Samoa, Australia, Fiji, French Polynesia, Guam, Kiribati, Marshall Islands, Micronesia, Nauru, New Caledonia, Niue, New Zealand, Northern Mariana Islands, Palau, Papua New Guinea, Samoa, Solomon Islands, Tonga, Tuvalu, Vanuatu.

7. Sunday

Give praise and worship to: Almighty God
Jesus Christ
Holy Spirit

Look back over your prayer requests this week and give thanks for the answered prayers.

Pray for the upcoming services this day.

DISCUSSION OF WARRIORS

Chapter 1

Samson

Samson was a feared warrior by the Philistines. At his wedding feast, the guests figured out his riddle that he had killed a lion with his bare hands so he killed thirty Philistines to provide clothes for the guests.[12] Later, when his wife was killed, he attacked and slaughtered many Philistines. When the Philistines persuaded the Israelites to hand him over, he attacked them and killed a thousand of them with the jawbone of a donkey.[13] At his death, he pushed down a temple killing three thousand Philistines inside.[14]

1. What is your favorite video game? Why?
2. Have you ever played a game where you had to rescue a hostage before?
3. Have you ever played a game where your team ran off and left you to defend home base? How does it make you feel?
4. Have you ever played as a medic trying to heal people up and unable to go off fighting?
5. Have you ever sacrificed yourself to save a teammate or to save a mission?
6. What does this mean? "Greater love has no one than this, that he lay down his life for his friends" (John 15:13 NIV).

---

[12] Judges 14.
[13] Judges 15.
[14] Judges 16:25–30.

Chapter 2

David

David was a shepherd boy who killed a bear and lion protecting his sheep. Later, he took five smooth stones and killed the giant Goliath, the champion of the Philistines, with his sling and then used the giant's own sword to cut off his head.[15] He was promoted in Saul's army to command a thousand men and was successful in his campaigns.[16] When Saul asked for a dowry of a hundred dead Philistines for his daughter to marry David, he killed two hundred Philistines.[17] He fought and saved the city of Keisha[18] and destroyed the Amalekites who stole his family from Ziglag.[19] He was crowned King of Judah and later Israel and defeated numerous countries that attacked Israel.

1. What is your favorite video warrior? Why?
2. What weapon does he/she use? How does he/she use it?
3. Draw a line to match the weapon with the correct warrior.

Yasaka	Sword/wide shield
Shumba Musiwa	Scimitar
Tempeste	Bow/dagger
Andrew	Tabar/breaching shield
Raven	Short sword/key
Fatima	Assegai
Vladislav	Trident/weighted net
Freddie	Short sword/claws
Hong Jiantou	Rapier
Ferdinand	Katana

---

[15] First Samuel 17.
[16] First Samuel 18:12.
[17] First Samuel 18:26.
[18] First Samuel 23:1–12.
[19] First Samuel 30.

4. What position is Jay trying out for?
5. Have you ever seen a movie that featured Roman soldiers? What were they famous for?
6. Can you match these warriors with their weapons in the Bible?

Samson (Judg. 15)   Nail and hammer
David (1 Sam. 17)   Sword, bow and arrow
Jael (Judg. 4)   Donkey's jawbone
Jonathan (1 Sam. 14)   Sword, torch, and trumpet
Gideon (Judg. 6–8)   Sling/staff

Did you pass that level? Now let's upgrade it. What about these?

Abishai (2 Sam. 23:18)   Bow and arrow/
                                  chariot/spear
Shamgar, son of Anath
(Judg. 3:31)   Left-handed dagger
Ehud (Judg. 3:12–30)   Club
Woman of Thebez (Judg. 9:53)   Spear
Jehu, King of Israel (2 Kings 9) Millstone
Benaiah, commander of David's   Ox goad
bodyguard (2 Sam. 23:20–23)

God called these warriors out for a purpose.

7. What has he called you to do?

Chapter 3

Jael

Not all warriors are men. Deborah was a judge in Israel and led Israel to revolt against Jabin. She and Barak led the Israelite army into battle, and when the Lord bogged down the iron chariots of Sisera in a storm, they won a mighty victory. Sisera tried to escape on foot, but when he came to Jael's tent, she invited him, gave him some milk, and covered him up. While he was sleeping, she hammered a tent peg through his temple into the ground, giving Israel deliverance.[20]

1. Have you heard of an incredible story where someone's life was saved and it didn't seem physically possible? Have you read where someone was able to lift something off someone that wasn't physically possible?

2. In Revelations (5:8), there are twenty-four elders before the Lamb. "Each one had a harp and they were holding golden bowls full of incense, which are the prayers of the saints." What smell do you think your prayers carry before God?

3. What games have you played before where you had a health, power, or supply gauge?

4. In this story, Jay saw a prayer gauge that measured the amount of prayer put into a request by the number of people praying and the time spent.

The Bible tells us to "pray continually" (1 Thess. 5:17 NIV). Does this mean we need to walk around with our eyes closed, praying out loud?

When Moses was praying for Joshua and the children of Israel in their battle with the Amalekites, they kept winning. When he stopped, they started losing.

Who came alongside him to help him keep praying and won the victory?

When have you asked friends to pray with you for a specific prayer request?

---

[20] Judges 4.

5. In this chapter, Brian is a man fighting an addiction that he never meant to enslave him. This is a hard fight.

What are some addictions people battle with?

Do you know some friends who struggle with addiction?

How can you pray for them and encourage them?

"Call to me and I will answer you and tell you great and unsearchable things you do not know" (Jer. 33:3 NIV).

Chapter 4

Shamgar

Shamgar, son of Anath, like Deborah, was another judge who was called on to rescue Israel. He took an oxgoad (probably an iron-tipped staff) and killed six hundred Philistines to save Israel.[21]

1. Jay enjoys hunting. Have you ever been hunting before? What have you hunted? Did you use a rifle or shotgun? Do you agree or disagree with the analogy that prayer is like a rifle?
2. What do you clean your weapon with? How do you clean your scope?
   Different cleaners or the same?
   Do you need to ask for forgiveness before you pray? Why?
3. Jonathan and his shield bearer climbed up a mountain and took out a Philistine outpost. Jonathan was a good fighter and a good archer. He practiced his archery for such a time as this. Jehu shot his opponent from a speeding bouncing chariot but could only have become this accurate from hours

---

[21] Judges 3:31.

of shooting. David knew if he was going to hit Goliath, he had to choose an aerodynamic rock to get the most velocity. For accurate precise prayers, what do you need to do?

4. Have you ever heard something negative that someone said or posted about you on Instagram, Snapchat, or text messaging? Maybe someone said something over Discord while you were playing a game or voted off a team. This can really hurt. The devil will try and use these comments to tear you down.

   But you are a child of the King, and your value is in Jesus. Since He loved you enough to die for you, you are incredibly valuable to Him.

5. What can you pray when Satan is trying to tear you down?

6. How can you prayer for someone in school who is being bullied and mocked?

Chapter 5

Ehud

When Eglon, the king of Moab, ruled over Israel, Ehud, the son of Gera the Benjamite, a left-handed man, strapped a foot and a half-long sword to his right thigh under his clothes. Most people are right-handed so guards generally checked your left hip. He carried the tribute from Israel to Eglon and told him he had a secret message. After Eglon sent his attendants out, Ehud said, "I have a message from God for you," and stabbed Eglon in his fat belly. He was so fat that the blade and handle went in and were covered with the fat so Ehud couldn't get it out. He escaped from the palace, raised an army from Ephraim, and killed over ten thousand Moabites in their successful revolt.[22]

1. In a video game, how have you highlighted a designated target like Ehud targeted Eglon?

---

[22] Judges 3:12–30.

Have you tagged it with a cursor, placed a box on it, or painted it with a laser?
In your prayers, how have you precisely pointed out a target that needs to be prayed over?
Do you write it down or type a note on your phone?

2. Do you have any friends who aren't believers?
How can you pray that they will believe in Jesus Christ?
Pray that they will not be distracted by life around them but realize their great need for a personal savior.

3. There are times when the hurt cuts so deep that there are no words left to pray. Who speaks for us when our prayers aren't answered as we wished and we are in such pain?
Although we may not see an answer to our anguished cries immediately, we know that Jesus hurts for us and wants to provide healing to our hearts. The Holy Spirit stores up each tear and sorrow, and one day, we know the answers will be revealed.

Chapter 6

Benaiah

Benaiah, son of Jehoiada, was a mighty man from Kabzeel. He killed two of Moab's top fighters, went into a pit on a snowy day to kill a lion, and with only a club, attacked a giant Egyptian armed with a spear and killed him. He was placed as the commander of David's bodyguard[23] and assisted Solomon in his coronation by executing those who conspired against Solomon.

1. Why is it that sometimes it is easier to accept Christ into your heart than it is to live for Him?
2. Why did Mrs. Samporn have a hard time getting rid of her spirit house?

---

[23] Second Samuel 23:20–23.

3. Why is it good to know what struggles a person might have after becoming a Christian?
4. Jay had to take a larger role in directing this battle to secure an enemy stronghold. What are the most famous generals in history?
5. Who is the best general or leader in a video game?
6. Can you match these top generals from the Bible with their victories?

Ehud (Judg. 3:12–30) Defeated the Philistines, Edomites, Ammonites, Arameans, and Syria.

Gideon (Judg. 6–8) With a smaller army defeated Absalom's larger army.

Joshua (Josh.) Defeated thousands of Midianites with three hundred men.

David (2 Sam. 8–10) Killed the king of Moab and led a revolt.

Joab (2 Sam. 18) Defeated the Amalekites, Jericho, and the kings of Canaan.

Chapter 7

Abishai

Abishai, the son of David's oldest sister, was close to David. When David went into Saul's camp and they stole Saul's spear and water jar, it was Abishai who accompanied him.[24] He was the brother of Joab, David's general, but also a fighter who killed three hundred men in one battle with his spear.[25] During one battle Ishbi-Benob, a Philistine giant carrying a spear that weighed three hundred shekels and a new sword said he would kill David. He fought his way to where an exhausted David was fighting, and it looked like he was

---

[24] Second Samuel 2:18.
[25] Second Samuel 23:18–19.

going to carry out his threat. However, Abishai cut his way through to David's side and killed the giant, saving David's life.[26]

1. What was the biggest boss fight you have ever had?
2. Who is the baddest fighter today?
3. Who was the toughest warrior in the Bible?
4. Match these mighty warriors with their victories.

Abishai (2 Sam. 23:18–19)	Killed a bear, lion, Goliath the giant, as well as 200 Philistines.
Josheb-Basshebeth (2 Sam. 23:8–17)	Killed 1,000 Philistines with a donkey's jawbone.
Eleazar, son of Dodai (2 Sam. 23 9–10)	Alone defeated the Philistines in the field of lentils.
Shammah (2 Sam. 23:11–12)	Killed 600 Philistines with an oxgoad.
Benaiah (2 Sam. 23:20–23)	Stood alone, defeated the Philistines at Pad Dammin with his hand frozen to his sword.
David (1 Sam. 17)	Killed 300 men with his spear, killed the giant Isbi-benob.
Samson (Judg. 15)	Killed 800 men at one time.
Shamgar, son of Anath (Judg. 3:31)	Killed two of Moab's top fighters, a lion in a pit, a giant Egyptian armed with a spear while he only had a club.

Chapter 8

Josheb-Basshebeth

Josheb-Basshebeth was the chief of David's three mighty men. He killed eight hundred men in one battle and three hundred in

---

[26] Second Samuel 21:15–17.

another. He fought alongside the other two mighty men—Eleazar, son of Dodai, and Shammah, son of Agee the Hararite—when they taunted the Philistines at Pas Dammim. The rest of the army fled, but the three of them fought alone until the Philistines were defeated. Eleazar's hand was frozen to his sword after the battle. Another time, the three of them snuck through enemy lines one night to get some good water from Bethlehem's well for David who missed his hometown water. David was so moved by the risk they took, he poured it out and wouldn't drink it.[27] Later, Josheb-Basshebeth was put in command of one of the army divisions that was in charge for the first month of the year.

1. Just like the Zimbabweans who praise God through the drought and the new borehole, can you praise God through the good and the bad times?
2. There are many things that can imprison us—old sins, memories, or traumatic events. Can you ask God to jailbreak you from these chains that bind you so that you can be released to a new life of joy?
3. It is good to see answers to prayers, to see the sick restored to health. Coronavirus has emphasized the uncertainty of life. But we can be certain that we know who the giver of life is. Do you have a journal where you write down your prayer requests daily? I urge you to do this, and you will be surprised at the amount of answered prayer once you start recording it.

Chapter 9

Jonathan

Jonathan, the son of Saul, first attacked an outpost of Philistines at Geba. Then he and his armor bearer climbed up the pass at Micmash to attack another outpost of Philistines, and the two of

---

[27] Second Samuel 23:8–17.

them killed twenty. This caused panic among the Philistines, and they were routed.[28] Jonathan was an incredible friend and loyal to David, no matter how many times Saul tried to kill David. On Mount Gilboa, alongside his brothers and father Saul, Jonathan died a warrior with his sword in his hand, fighting the Philistines.[29]

1. Have you ever been picked out of group to do a job? How did it make you feel?

   Embarrassed to be singled out?

   Frustrated because you didn't want to do it?

   Honored that the boss thought you were the only one able to do it?

2. Have you had a family member get sick and they didn't get well?

   When have you prayed and God not answered your prayer like you had hoped?

   This can hurt as we don't know why this happened.

   But we know who wins in the end. We can continue to pray and fight for those who are hurting today, even if the results aren't always what we want.

   We know that Jesus has won the final victory and we have the opportunity to participate in the cleanup duty before he returns.

3. Jay was picked to do a job.

   These warriors that we have discussed were picked for a special task.

   I know that God has a special purpose and a unique job for you.

Are you willing to accept the warrior's challenge he has for you?

---

[28] First Samuel 14:1–14.
[29] First Samuel 31:1–6.

ACKNOWLEDGMENTS

Thank you to those who shared their testimonies with me and helped me with this story; Steve and Judy Anderson, Shirley Randall, Tim Lacy, Sheila Harkins, Susie Hansen, Rissa Harkins Edwards, Matt and Miles Randall, Kim P. Davis, Yuji and Jerri Ann Yasaka, John Davis, Paul Murphy, Duane Hughes, Janet Erwin, Brett Burleson and others in closed countries.

CPSIA information can be obtained
at www.ICGtesting.com
Printed in the USA
BVHW080539191021
619151BV00001B/2